Books by Jane O'Brien

The White Pine Trilogy:

The Tangled Roots of Bent Pine Lodge #1

The Dunes & Don'ts Antiques Emporium #2

The Kindred Spirit Bed & Breakfast #3

The Lighthouse Trilogy:

The 13th Lighthouse #1

The Painted Duck #2

Owl Creek #3

The Unforgettables:

Ruby and Sal #1

Maisy and Max #2

Ivy and Fox #3

Georgy and Jack #4

Pinecones

and

Promises

Merry Christmas!
Jane O'Brien

Connect with Jane O'Brien
www.authorjaneobrien.com
http://www.amazon.com/author/obrienjane
www.facebook.com/janeobrien/author/

Contact: authorjaneobrien@gmail.com

Book Cover: SelfPubBookCovers.com/ RLSather

This book is dedicated to my parents, who have both gone on to be with our Lord and Savior. I never knew two people more excited about Christmas in my life. Even though we did not have much money, Dad would save all year long, to make sure there was enough money for gifts and food. And Mom would pour her heart and soul into making everything just right, from homemade gifts such as knitted sweaters and mittens, to buying whatever was popular for a child or teen at the time. They would invite different family members over every year to share Christmas dinner, and my mother would set the table with her best china and crystal, serving everyone turkey with all of the fixings, making sure everyone had what they needed, and probably eating cold food herself. Words of love were never spoken, but by example and deeds I always knew I was loved. I am proud that I had such caring parents who truly had the spirit of Christmas within them.

Table of Contents

Don't make rash promises, and don't be hasty in
bringing matters before God. After all, God is in heaven,
and you are here on earth. So let your words be few.

Ecclesiastes 5:2

Pinecones

And

Promises

Jane O'Brien

Chapter One

The hustle and bustle outside the plate glass window would probably look to any casual observer as a happy Christmas scene from a Hallmark movie. The snow was gently falling and settling on the holiday decorations, while at the same time leaving a fluffy white coat on the ground. Some lights on the strings which were hanging over doors and windows were completely covered in cottony poofs, so that only a hazy colored glow was showing through. Nate was focused on a woman wearing a bright red wool coat. She reminded him so much of someone he once knew. An ache of loneliness suddenly overcame him. He noticed her curly brown hair popping out wildly underneath her knitted beret. She was with a small child, maybe five or six; obviously a girl because of her bright pink jacket. They were looking at a store window display, pointing and laughing; no doubt the child was showing her what she wanted for Christmas. The woman bent over to place a kiss on the child's cheek, then took the little hand in hers as they turned to walk down the street. Standing on his toes and leaning into the window, Nate craned to see them until they were out of his view.

It had always been this way for him -- watching others enjoy the holiday season, without actually taking part himself. This had been the norm since he was a child. He had learned to adjust. It no longer hurt -- that emotion had been shelved away deep within himself. Now he felt nothing but a dull ache at something lost that he had no knowledge of. As a matter of fact, most of his emotions had been deadened a long time ago, and lately, more than ever, he had been coasting through life – doing what was expected, nothing more, nothing less.

Nathan Finnegan was a very likable guy, mid-thirties, just starting a new job, and good looking to boot. His dark hair set off his deep brown eyes. He seemed to have a perpetual tan, even without the use of tanning booths; his perfect white teeth often flashed when he laughed out loud, leaving people to assume he was a happy person, even though he did not feel that sentiment in his soul.

This time of year was particularly difficult for Nate. He had to work extra hard to cover up his apathy for Christmas. He was not a 'bah humbug' type of person, and did not want people to perceive him that way. He just truly didn't care one way or the other if it was Christmas or not. Since he never had any specific plans, he was usually quite surprised when the annual date in December neared and suddenly decorations of green and red began popping up in his friends' homes and on his coworkers' desks. Once the holiday spirit had infected most everyone around him, he would pretend to be a part of it and respond with the usual greeting of 'Merry Christmas.' He went out for drinks with his co-workers and took part in the normal chatter of what they were shopping for and what their kids wanted for Christmas. When pressed about his plans, he would be quite vague. The usual response was that nothing had been decided yet. Some years, he said, were spent at his mother's house and some years they had gone to his sister's place. This year his sister was pregnant, so they were waiting to see if the baby came before or after Christmas. Several people congratulated him on becoming an uncle soon, and one young woman even asked what he was planning to buy the soon-to-be niece or nephew for a gift. She had been interested in Nate for quite a while, and even though he had not returned her feelings, she persisted by asking if she could help him choose something. She would be happy to go shopping with him, she said. Nate managed to put her off by telling her he planned to wait to see if it was a boy or girl, since his sister had not wanted to know in advance, and did not know herself.

The truth of it all, was that Nate didn't even have a sister. He was an only child. Dropped off at a fire station on a cold snowy night one Christmas Eve, wrapped in swaddling clothes just like the baby Jesus, and left in a basket outside of the firehouse door, so he was told. Once discovered he was rushed, lights flashing and sirens screaming, to the local hospital in Fort Wayne, Indiana, for a checkup. From there he was placed into temporary foster care and then adoption. Nate's adopted parents had been on a wait list for quite a while, so when the baby became available, his mother, Stacy, was more than eager to claim him. All of her friends had children. She thought it was time for them, too. His father, Gary Finnegan, had been having some difficulties at work and felt that this *wasn't* the right time. But his wife was very excited, so he didn't want to tell her they should probably go to the bottom of the list and begin the wait again. That way they would be more prepared financially when the time came.

The moment the couple took the previously unnamed baby home, Nate's father knew it was a mistake. He was not cut out to be a parent, he said. He couldn't stand the constant crying, and the middle of the night feedings. Once they got past that colicky stage and the teething began, he would get so tense with all of the fussing and drool that he would often walk out, leaving Nate's mother to handle the situation alone. Stacy was frustrated with her mothering abilities, since nothing came naturally to her. Soon she looked for reasons to be away from home, also. She volunteered at the church and joined a book club, hiring a babysitter regularly, even on grocery shopping days. After the couple signed the formal adoption papers, Stacy got a job and put Nate in daycare, but when she came home from work, already exhausted from a long day, she began to resent the fact that she still had to take care of her baby, when all she wanted was a warm hot bath and some alone time.

Stacy demanded that Gary help out with their child, but he refused. He said he was exhausted from work, too, and besides he didn't know anything about children. And if he were to admit it, Nate scared him. He was like a little alien from outer space. The tension at home was so bad, that Gary's eye began to wander. There was a cute young thing at the office that had shown an interest in him. When she invited him to go to the bar with her, he didn't see the harm in having just one drink after work. It wasn't long before it became routine for the two of them to leave work together. After a time, they started to stay later and later, having way more than their promised 'one drink.' Amy was happy to be his sounding board, she said. She felt so sorry for Gary. Things were so rough at home. She would lean closer while he talked and gently place her hand on his thigh for comfort, her scoop-neck top exposing everything she intended to show. And then one night, she invited him to her place, and he went eagerly without any guilt, whatsoever. The sex was wild and crazy, and best of all, there was not a crying child in the background to interrupt their pleasures. Over time, Amy convinced him that she would make a much better wife. She didn't like kids, she said. He would never have to go through that again with her. It sounded real good to him, sex whenever he wanted it and a woman to drink with, so he left Stacy and moved in with Amy. His wife filed for divorce shortly after.

Stacy was not surprised with Gary's actions, but furious just the same. Now she was left to take care of the kid all by herself. The Court made sure Gary paid his share of child support, but he made it clear to Stacy that even though the kid was legally his, he was not his flesh and blood. He would be a money donor only until the child was eighteen, because he was forced to be, but he had no other interest in the boy. Nate never saw his father again, and when he was old enough and learned the story of his adoption and why his father had left them, it finally made sense to him why he did not have a family like the other kids. After that, he never thought about Gary again. His mother kept whatever child support money came her way to herself to pay the bills, and she never said a word as to whether it was enough or if it even came regularly.

Christmases were sparse. They usually just had a very small table tree, because Nate begged for one so he could be like the other kids. He would get one or two presents, sometimes wrapped and sometimes not. On occasion the gift would still be in the original shopping bag. Sometimes one of his mother's boyfriends would buy him a small gift, but most of her men weren't even aware that she had a child.

When he was young, Nate would sometimes make a card for his mother out of construction paper, and later when he was old enough to get a job, he would buy her an inexpensive piece of jewelry, but she never showed much enthusiasm, so after a while he stopped buying or making gifts. When he returned to school after the holidays and heard the kids talk about what they had done with their parents and what gifts they had received, he would make up stories to match theirs. He was careful not to exaggerate too much so his story sounded plausible, and as time went on, he got really good at blending in with the others with his Christmas enthusiasm. And that's where he was today. Nothing had changed. Even when he had had a few girlfriends who had insisted on decorating his apartment for him, or buying him elaborate gifts, he felt nothing. If he felt nothing, when he was eventually let down, there would be no pain.

On his seventeenth birthday, after graduation, Nate started proceedings to emancipate himself. The filing fees and court costs were high, but he had been saving everything he earned at his car wash job for quite a while, and with the help of a sympathetic attorney who offered him a pro bono rate, he was able to make it happen. When he told his mother what he was doing, she never objected once. He even saw a sign of relief flicker across her face. Without her objection, their separation went through the court system easily.

Once he was his own man, he realized he would need to find a job that paid well. He loved being physical and outdoors, so when he saw an ad online for a job at a Christmas tree farm in Michigan, he applied. Unlike what most people think, farming Christmas trees is a year-round occupation. There's always something to be trimmed or sheared as it is known, or fertilized, or sprayed for bugs; and there's the irritating weed control. The never-ending job of cutting down and getting rid of the old trees that had never sold took lots of time as well as replanting young ones. Christmas trees could take up to 7 to 10 years before they would be offered for sale.

Working outdoors at the tree farm was exactly what Nate was suited for. He loved the physical labor, and best of all, room and board was provided. He lived in a small cabin with two other guys. They ate two large meals a day in the large farmhouse at a communal table and sandwiches were provided in the field at noon. His first few months were idyllic, but he quickly became aware of the fact that he did need an education in order to advance in the world. He saved all of his weekly wages by staying to himself. He never went out or partied with the other young workers, so eventually he had enough money to be able to apply to community college. He discovered he was good with numbers, so he thought the logical thing to do was to get a degree in accounting. Nate continued to work at the tree farm while he took a few classes at a time. He kept his head on straight, was well-liked by everyone, and did his job efficiently.

Then one day the tree farmer's daughter came home from college over spring break. As Nate allowed himself to remember that particular time in his life, something he very rarely did, a sharp pain coursed across the top of his head. He brushed his hand over his forehead, trying to rub the flashing images away, but instead he saw everything clearly the way it was back then.

Chapter Two

Sixteen Years Earlier

The sun had been beating on Nate's back all day. It was still early spring, but the temperatures were screaming mid-summer. He had been moving from tree to tree through the rows with the pruners in hand as he shaped the fresh new greenery into perfect cones. Bugs were biting, sap was sticking to his clippers, and sweat was dripping down his front and back, leaving huge wet stains on his sleeveless tank top. His exposed arms rippled with muscles as he worked. Stopping a moment to adjust his dew rag which had gotten caught on a branch, Nate took the chance to stand up straight and stretch a little. He rubbed his lower back a moment at the top of his jeans and took a long drink from his water bottle. The moisture that had collected on the outside ran down the front of his shirt. The work was hard but he was used to it; in fact, he loved every minute of it. He squinted into the sun, about to call out to Freddy, the owner's son and his best friend on the farm. He was down the line a bit, working on the next row. Freddy was three years older than Nate, and even though he was the owner's son, he worked equally hard so the two got along very well. At the moment Freddy had his arms wrapped around a very shapely young woman, whom he had just picked up, twirling around until she squealed. With a smirk, Nate watched as Freddy went in for a long kiss, which at first was a "happy-to-see-you" kiss, but soon turned into something that no voyeur should be watching. Claire was Freddy's longtime girlfriend, and as Freddy had told him, they had been a couple since they were kids in elementary school. Apparently, she was home from college, and that meant one thing – so was her best friend and Freddy's sister, Molly.

Nate searched the rows for a sign of her, but could see nothing. They had met briefly the day he first arrived here, but she had spent the rest of the summer visiting relatives in Colorado. She had returned just in time to leave for college, so he hadn't seen her since. On that one meeting when their eyes had met, it would have been obvious to anyone who caught the look that sparks were flying. Nate had quickly made an excuse of needing to get settled in, and left. He was embarrassed by his behavior now as he thought back on it. He was almost hoping *not* to run into her again, but just as he bent back to work, he felt a ping on his back. Looking down at his feet, he saw a small pinecone that had bounced off of him. And then another one, larger this time, bounced off his arm.

"What in the world?" Right before he turned he heard a giggle. When he spun around he was looking right at her, the most beautiful girl he had ever laid eyes on and the one he saw nightly in his dreams. She had brown hair thick with wild curls. It was tied back at the nape of her neck, but even though the elastic band was doing its best, there was no way she would ever be able to contain the coils. Her eyes were light grey, a color he had never seen on anyone before. She was petite and put together in all the right places – round and soft where she needed to be, and firm where she should be. She was laughing at him; he ducked his head in embarrassment.

"So, you're back," he said, and immediately thinking he sounded stupid.

"Yup. Just for spring break, though. Sorry for the pinecones. I couldn't resist. I was walking through the trees, trying to give my brother and Claire some privacy. They couldn't wait to see each other again." Molly studied the young man in front of her. He was the perfect subject for a monthly calendar picture. He had grown a little taller than when she had seen him last, and it looked like the hard work had produced a few more muscles. He was gorgeous and everything she had always been attracted to in a boy. She avoided looking at him while he was looking at her, so he would not know how weak in the knees she was just being near him. She had secretly been dreaming of him for months, but she had not breathed a word of him to anyone at school. Even Claire thought she wasn't interested. They all knew how she felt about being raised on the farm in Holly. She couldn't wait to get away from all of the work and the small town atmosphere. She would not allow any kind of attraction to deter her from her plan to move to a big city.

"You were right to give them space. They just disappeared into the heavier tree line." Nate studied the ground, then dared to look at her through a squint. The sun was at her back, making it difficult to see her, so he casually moved a little to another side of the tree that he was working on. As he had hoped, she moved with him. "How have you been, Molly?" There, he had dared to say her name.

"I'm fine. School is a bore, but that's to be expected. U of M is huge, but I love it there. There's always so much activity -- not like this no-nothing town."

Nate laughed. "Hey, it's not boring here. We've got plenty of fresh air and nature, and we're only an hour from big city activity in Detroit. There's always so much to do. Of course, I don't usually take advantage of it; I'm more of a home-body."

Nate couldn't believe his luck at the chance to be with her. He loved talking to her and hearing the sound of her voice; it gave him an opportunity to study her face. He didn't think he could ever get enough of watching her pouty lips move over those pearly white teeth, and that little dimple at the side of her mouth that jumped at certain words. His heart was pounding at the thought of what he could do to her given a chance. "Want to sit in the shade for a minute?"

Molly glanced back towards the aisle she had come from. There was no sign of her brother and her friend. "I guess, I should stay away from that area for a while," she said, gesturing over her shoulder. "Okay, but somewhere away from the clippings. I hate pinesap!"

"Well, now I know what you hate. This town, this farm, and pinesap. What do you love?" he asked, as they moved to an oak tree on the edge of the farm line.

"Believe it or not, I love Christmas, even though that means selling Christmas trees. My brothers always had to do the cutting and bailing for the customers, but I stayed in the barn with a heater and the cash register. Mom and I make wreaths and we sell those, too. I love the creativity. But mostly, I like to decorate the house with lights and garland. And I'm crazy about Christmas music – all kinds, old and new, pop and classical." She noticed a blankness cross over his face. "This will be your first Christmas at the farm, won't it?"

"Yup."

"What do you normally do? I mean, this year, you'll have to stay here to work, but what about

Christmas Eve and Christmas Day? Where will you go?"

This was the part that Nate always hated. He began to make up a story, as he usually did, but when he looked into her eyes, something made him tell the truth about the holidays for the first time in his life. "I don't have anywhere to go, but that's okay. I'm not really into Christmas."

"What? You're kidding! Everyone loves Christmas! Don't you have any family? Oh, I'm sorry, that was rude. I'm asking too many questions."

"No, it's okay. No, I really don't have anyone that I want to share the day with, but I've been on my own for a while now, so it's fine with me. I always look forward to some quiet time alone."

"Why, that's not Christmas, at all! No one should be alone. You'll spend it with us. I'll tell Mom."

"No, please don't. I don't want to intrude. It's a family thing, and I would be out of place. Besides, why are we even talking about this? It's only March! We've got a long way to go until Christmas."

Molly laughed. "You're right, I got ahead of myself. It's just that's it's my favorite time of year, so I think everyone should love it, too."

"Molly! I'm leaving!" came the call from down the row.

"Oh, that's Claire. I'd better get going." Molly held Nate's gaze for a moment. He found it difficult to pull his eyes away. She took his hand, and caressed her fingers over his knuckles. A bolt of electricity ran through him. "It was nice talking to you, Nate," she said softly. "I hope we can do it again sometime."

Nate gulped. "Yeah, me too."

Then she turned and ran to meet Freddy and Claire, leaving him wanting more – so much more.

Chapter Three

Day in and day out Nate worked on the farm, doing exactly what he was told. He was easygoing, always on time, and very reliable. He soon became the favorite of the Sparks family at Pine Haven Farm. Cora Sparks, known to everyone as Mom, took a special interest in Nate. She made sure that he ate right, she sometimes slipped an extra cookie or two in his lunch sack, and one time when he was sick with the flu, she cared for him like she would her own son. She watched as the young man struggled to work at the farm and attend college at the same time. He selected night classes whenever they were available, but once in a while he would ask for special permission to leave the farm for a few hours because he needed to attend a class or lecture in the afternoon. Duane Sparks began to think of him fondly, as well. He was pleased with how well he worked with Freddy and the other hands. When Nate and Freddy were in the field together, a lot of work got done. Nate kept Freddy in good spirits with his joking around and singing. So when Molly came home for the summer, he was not the least bit concerned that the four young people – Freddy and Claire, and Nate and Molly – began to spend time together. Nate was more than thrilled that Molly had been so eager to see him again that May.

"Nate, are you up for a movie tonight?" asked Freddy. "I thought the four of us could go out together."

"You did? Does Molly approve?" asked Nate, hoping against hope.

Freddy laughed. "It was her idea. She said she thought it would be good for Claire and me to have a little fun, but I think she was more interested in being paired up with you."

"Really? Sure, that sounds great. But Freddy, what do you think about me going on a date with your sister? Is it okay with you?"

"Are you crazy? Of course, and Mom and Dad are good with it, too. They wouldn't have much to say about it anyway, because when Molly makes up her mind about something, no one can change it. And I think she has already made up her mind about you."

Nate blushed at what he said, dipped his head in embarrassment, and grinned at the thought that he might have a chance to be with Molly someday. He had dreamed of being a part of this family since the day he first met them. He knew he was getting ahead of himself. He had not yet had a real date with Molly since they met, but tonight could be the start of something that could change his life.

The days had been unseasonably warm, but the nights were still cool, as they often were at this time of year in Michigan. Nate dressed casually, wearing jeans and a tee shirt, but nonetheless he agonized over his choice. Was the tee shirt acceptable, did she expect more, should he use cologne or not, should he just towel dry his hair or use gel?

Nate had no idea that at the exact same time he was struggling to find a way to please Molly, she was going through the same process. Jeans or skirt? Makeup or clean face? Straighten her hair or let the curls run free? In the end nothing mattered, because as soon as they each laid eyes on each other, all worries went out the window. Molly saw the best looking boy she had ever seen, and from Nate's perspective no one could ever top Molly -- she was drop-dead gorgeous.

Freddy drove them into Pontiac so they could go to a larger movie studio. They took Highway 59 and back roads, which gave Nate and Molly the opportunity to be in the backseat together for about 40 minutes. They started out quietly talking about school and classes, and soon they were laughing and chatting like they had known each other all of their lives. When they arrived at the 25 movie-screen theater complex, Freddy grabbed Claire's hand, and Nate reached for Molly's. He was thrilled when she smiled at him, and leaned into him a little so their arms were brushing together. It gave him the courage to throw his arm around her shoulders during the movie, and Molly followed suit by snuggling closer, laying her head on his shoulder. Nate wasn't sure what the plot was about, but he wished the movie would never end. When the evening was over, instead of dropping Claire off at her house first, Freddy took Molly and Nate home and then took Claire home. It was obvious he wanted time alone with his girl.

"I had a great time, Nate," Molly said shyly.

"Me, too. I'd love to do it again. What do you think?"

"Sure, that would be wonderful."

Nate noticed her shiver a little. "Are you cold? Want my jacket?"

Molly laughed. "No, silly, we're home. I can go in and get a warmer coat."

"Do you want to -- go in, I mean? Would you like to stay out a while longer?" asked Nate, hoping to prolong the evening.

"Uh, what if I would? What then?" she flirted.

Thinking quickly, he said, "Let's make a fire in the pit. It's a beautiful night. I can grab my warm jacket and meet you back here in a few minutes."

"That's sounds great." She grinned and spontaneously kissed him on the cheek.

"Okay, then. Uh, okay. See you in a minute."

Molly ran inside, yelling, "Mom, I'm home. We're going to sit out by the fire for a while."

"Okay, dear. Have fun."

By the time Molly had freshened up, and put on a different coat, Nate was already back and had started working on the fire. The intoxicating smell of the pine branches burning, and the sound of the pine pitch popping was relaxing and cozy. Sparks from green wood rose to the sky, dancing like fireflies. The two settled in side by side on the yard swing, which had been built close to the fire pit. Molly put her head back on Nate's arm and gazed at the stars. "Look at the sky, Nate. Just look at it. I've never seen the stars so bright." Could anything be more perfect, she wondered?

"Molly, what's in your future? What happens after college?" asked Nate, hoping he wasn't moving too quickly, but he just had to know.

"I've decided to go into horticulture. I've always loved plants, flowers as well as trees, and I thought I could learn something that might benefit the family business. But mostly, I'd love to work in a greenhouse or do landscape work, maybe even be a landscape architect. I'm not sure about that last part, yet."

"Wow, you have big dreams. I had no idea."

"What about you?" she asked.

"Well, my plans aren't quite formulated yet. I take it one day at a time, but I seem to be pretty good with numbers, so I might just do two years and get an associate's degree in accounting."

Molly laughed. "Doing taxes? That does not sound like you one bit. You couldn't stand being cooped up in an office."

Nate joined in the laughter. "You're probably right. I do love being outside. Maybe someday I can own a farm of my own, like this one. I sure have learned a lot since I started here. Anything's possible, right?"

Molly tipped back her head and looked at him with her big grey eyes, and said softly, "Yes, Nate. Anything *is* possible." Then she moved slightly, just enough to offer him her lips, which he took full advantage of. This kiss was different than any other he had ever tasted. Shock waves careened through his whole body. Molly wrapped her arms around his neck and pulled him in closer. They moved along with the swaying of the swing, the world spiraling into space, as their two souls ached to be one. When they finally pulled apart, not one word was spoken. Nate gently caressed Molly's cheek, wrapped his fingers in a few curls, and then with one last kiss, he took her hand and walked her to the door, where they shared another moment of bliss in each other's arms.

Once Molly was inside, Nate put out the fire by separating the small pieces of wood and tossing water on the embers. The hiss and steam that rose in a hazy cloud carried with it his prayer about his feelings for Molly. As young as he was, he already knew she would be the only woman he would ever want for the rest of his life.

As Molly stepped inside the door she couldn't help but sigh. Her mother had been discreetly looking out the window at the two young lovers. It was her habit to keep a close watch on her children. She smiled at the happiness her daughter brought in with her.

"Well, someone had a good time."

"Oh hi, Mom. I did. I really did. Nate and I have so much in common, we can't seem to stop talking. I really hated to come in." She blushed at the thought of the last few kisses, the real reason she didn't want to come in.

"He seems like a nice enough boy, but we don't know a lot about him yet. Just be careful, okay?"

"Oh, Mom. I'm eighteen now. I can take care of myself. Don't worry. And besides, maybe we need to get to know him a little better anyway, as an employee, I mean."

"Yes, of course, as an employee," Cora chuckled. "How about if we invite him in for dinner with the family after church on Sunday?"

"That would be awesome. Thanks, Mom. I'm sure Freddy will love having his friend at the table."

"Yes, Freddy. Mmm hmm. Where is that brother of yours, anyway?"

"Oh, he decided to drop Claire off last. I think they're getting serious."

"I thought so, too. I'm glad for him, but she's still pretty young. I hope they've thought things through."

"Well, I for one am going to stay out of it. If it doesn't work between them, I don't want to lose my best friend."

"Wise decision. Now, off to bed, we've got a long day ahead of us tomorrow."

"Really?" whined Molly. "Even on spring break? Can't I sleep in a little?"

"Just a little, but we don't want to wait too long. The malls might sell out of everything before we get there," said Cora with a twinkle in her eye.

"Shopping? I'll be up no later than 9!" Molly kissed her mother on the cheek and happily ran up the stairs.

Cora, smiled to herself at the wonderment of how her daughter could so easily bounce between being a woman in love and a girl-child. It was a magical time of her life, and Cora didn't want to miss a moment of it.

Chapter Four

That Sunday, Nate was thrilled to find himself seated at the Sparks' dinner table. He had never been around a family that was close. He was in awe at the teasing and camaraderie. He had never experienced anything like it. One minute they were passing food around, and the next they were in a spirited political debate. Even though there were various opinions offered on the state of the world, it never got heated. After about fifteen minutes of politics, Cora demanded they change the subject.

"Now, someone tell me about themselves – no politics and no work. I don't want to hear the word Christmas tree. Molly, why don't you go first?"

Molly proceeded to tell a few things about her classes and professors and what she planned on taking next year to go towards her major. She left out stories about the frat parties that some of the girls went to. So far she had avoided them, but the peer pressure was strong. She hoped she would be able to say no, but she had to admit to being curious a bit.

Next, Freddy told a story about something he had heard on his latest visit to the hardware store.

"Freddy, you know better. That sounds like gossip to me. Let's not go there. Nate, how about you? We don't know anything about your family. You haven't been back to visit since you started to work here."

"Cora," added Duane, "that's the boy's private business. You don't need to answer, son."

"No, that's okay, Mr. Sparks. I don't mind." Nate started out to make up one of his famous stories, but he glanced at Molly and suddenly had a strong desire to tell this great family the truth. "You see, I have no one. Well, I do, sort of, but not any longer."

"I don't understand," said Molly.

Nate proceeded to tell them about being left at the fire station as a baby, and then being adopted by parents who didn't really want him. Once he got to the part about the divorce and then being left alone a lot, he began to see pity in Cora's eyes, and almost changed his story to make it more pleasant. Freddy, on the other hand, was fascinated.

"How did you handle that, man? Did you see your father often or just for birthdays and Christmases?"

"No, days like those were pretty much ignored. I never saw my dad after the divorce and Mom struggled to pay the bills, so there were no parties or gifts. It was like I was living in a vacuum. Most of the time she barely talked to me. I took care of myself and went to school every day. I knew my only way out was to get an education. When I graduated, I applied for emancipation, and was granted it just before I came here. So, I'm my own man now, and I don't feel like I owe them anything."

Duane pounded his fist on the table. "And you shouldn't! Who does that to a child? People place their children into the adoption system with the thought that they will receive a better home than they would have been able to offer. Even though you were abandoned, I'm sure your mother thought she was doing the best thing for you. That just makes me angry. I'm sorry, son."

When Nate glanced at Molly, he could see tears in her eyes. Now he was uncomfortable. This is exactly why he never told anyone about his past.

"Don't worry. I'm fine. I managed to get through it, and now I have a great job, I've met this wonderful Sparks family," his eyes crinkled with joy, "and I'm going to college. It's more than I ever thought was possible. I'm a happy guy." He shoved in a large bite of his mashed potatoes.

"You are amazing," said Cora, wiping her eyes. "Look, I had no idea about your family. The other guys go home on Sunday, but I always thought you liked to be alone. I'm sorry. From now on Sunday dinners are with us, no matter if Freddy and Molly are here. We want you to feel part of the family."

Nate was so choked up that he was speechless for a few minutes. "I don't know what to say. I certainly never meant to tell you this for sympathy, but I would love to be a part of your family dinners. Thank you."

Molly got up from her chair and kissed him on the cheek right in front of her family. If Nate had known that telling the truth would have brought this response, he would have done it a long time ago.

Spring break was over too quickly and the young lovers found it difficult to part. They made promises to stay in touch regularly, and promises to date exclusively. While Molly was in college, she wrote often, since Nate did not have a computer or a smart phone. He had, however, purchased a prepay phone so he could keep in touch with her, but his minutes were limited. Once in a while he would talk to her from the landline phone in the farmhouse, but her family was always nearby and they couldn't be as free with their declarations of love. Nate worked harder than ever to show this family that he was worthy of their daughter. He even began attending church with them, and afterward he would go to the farmhouse for dinner where he would rave about the meals and help with the dishes. Cora was crazy about him, and Duane enjoyed having him around.

Suddenly, the end of the school year had arrived, and it was time for Molly to come home for the summer. Nate could hardly wait. He had been whittling a pinecone as a reminder of how she had tossed them at his back. He hoped she would take it back to school with her in the fall and remember him whenever she looked at it.

Molly could hardly wait to be back in Nate's arms and receive his kisses. When she pulled into the farmhouse driveway, he was waiting for her on the porch, leaning against a post, his baseball cap pulled low over his eyes, so as not to give away too much of his emotions. She barely had time to shut off the engine before she opened the car door, squealed her joy as she ran across the hard-packed dirt, and then with a leap, she wrapped her arms around him. They did not care one bit if the family saw them kiss.

"Molly, I missed you so much," Nate whispered into her curls. She smelled so good, he could hold her like this forever.

"Me, too, Nate. I didn't think school would ever end."

"Aren't you going to give your mother a hug?" laughed Cora, as she opened the screen door and stepped onto the porch.

"Sorry, Mom." Molly hugged her mother tightly. When she was in love, that feeling spilled over to anyone who was around. She glanced at her father, who was patiently waiting for his turn.

"Welcome home, baby girl." Molly loved the feeling of her father's strong arms. It was then that she realized why she loved Nate so. He had the same muscular back and arms that her father had developed after years of cutting, dragging, and lifting trees. Freddy had the same muscles, too. That was why Nate had felt so familiar right from the beginning, because whenever she snuggled close, she always felt safe with him.

From the day she first arrived home, the summer was filled with activity. During the day the boys worked in the field, while Molly helped her mother can fruits and vegetables. Sometimes she was allowed to catch up on some reading for her next year's syllabus. She had made a change in her major because she was now planning to become a teacher, perhaps high school biology and especially botany. Curled up on the porch swing, she listened to the bluejays' raucous calls; a cardinal sang to his mate from his perch in the tall pines. She had never enjoyed living on the farm in Holly so much in her entire life. Nate had given her a new way to look at the world. She hugged herself and thought about a future with him. But what began as a dreamy smile turned into a slight frown. The picture in her mind's eye was that of a farm wife and mother. Always so much work to do -- never ending work. A husband who always needed something, kids who always needed something, and those trees were forever and always demanding on the family time.

"Well, maybe Nate won't want to be a tree farmer," said Molly to herself. "It's just a temporary job, right?"

"What was that?" asked her mother, as she sat down in the rocker next to Molly.

"I was just wondering if Nate had ever told you about his future plans."

"Like what? After college?"

"Yes, like what will he do when he graduates? Does he plan on staying here? I can't imagine that."

"Maybe you should ask him yourself, dear. I would have thought you would have covered that subject already."

"No, no we haven't, not really."

Cora studied her daughter's face. She knew all too well the power of love. She had had plans of her own. She had wanted to be an artist in some creative area, but as soon as she met Duane, it was all over. Her life went wherever he wanted to go, and that was tree farming. And wasn't that what the Bible said to do? Cleave unto your husband? Wither thou goest, I will go? Where thou lodgest, I will lodge? These were things she had been taught all of her life. So Cora had been a good wife and had followed her husband's dreams for the family, and in the end it had all worked out. It was all part of God's plan, after all. She was happy, her family was wonderful, and they were all cared for, but every once in a while, she wondered what might have been.

"You know, Molly, I know you have strong feelings for Nate, but you are very young, yet. There's no need to make big decisions about your future now. Give it time. There's a reason why we need to go through courtship first, then followed by an engagement before marriage. It gives you time to sort things out, and make sure you are choosing the right person. This is someone you will spend the rest of your life with. Don't get me wrong, I love Nate, but you are my daughter and you come first. I'm just saying you should be careful and make your decision wisely."

Molly bit her lower lip. Right now, not being with Nate seemed to be out of the question, but little doubts had crept in on occasion, lately. She knew her mother was right. She must be truthful with herself and very careful. She didn't want to be one of those girls who got married at eighteen, had a baby by nineteen, and was saddled down for the rest of her life with a brood of kids and a demanding husband. "Thanks Mom, you've given me something to think about."

"Now, don't get me wrong. Have fun with Nate this summer. That's the only way you'll get to know him and see both sides of him, because believe me, there is always more to a man than what you see when you're first dating. Make sure you have things in common and that your goals and plans for the future are aligned. Then once you know him well, you'll be able to make the right choice. He's a good boy, sweet and kind. From my point of view you can't go wrong, but it's your life. So do what is right for you."

"You're absolutely right. I'll take that advice."

"What was that?" asked Cora playfully. "Did my teenage daughter say I was right? Did she say she would take my advice? Where's the recorder? I need to save this for posterity."

The mother and daughter walked inside to prepare supper. Molly squeezed her mother's hand. She *would* pay attention to the words she had been lovingly given. She would be looking at Nate in a new way, from this day on. She would watch and be careful.

The summer went flying by. The two young couples spent all of their free time together. They went swimming and boating, they waterskied and hiked, they saw movies in Flint and concerts in Detroit. Nate and Molly looked forward to alone time when they could talk about their dreams of the future. The Sunday dinners with the family continued and Nate had never been happier in his life.

Nate was walking ahead of Molly on a trail to the beach of a small inland lake, when he felt a ping on his back and knew immediately what it was. He turned around and got a baby pinecone right on the top of his head. Looking on the ground, he spotted what Molly had been using. They were everywhere, tiny little pinecones, just right for tossing. Laughing, he scooped up a handful. "You're in for it now, Miss Molly." She ducked as he lobbed one at her.

"Ha! You missed. Ouch! That one connected, all right. Here, take that, and that."

"Okay, truce, please, mercy!" Taking advantage of the fact that she was bent over with her giggles, Nate reached her in record time and scooped her into his arms. They were completely alone on the path, so he pulled her into his arms and tasted her sweet lips. Molly molded her body to his and returned the kiss with eagerness. Her fingers stroked the side of his face, while his were caressing her back. Molly wished he would never stop, but at the same time she was afraid of being discovered.

"Nate, we should stop," she gasped in between kisses. "Someone will come soon."

"No, I need more, I want more." Nate's breath was short and ragged. "Molly, I think I --"

"Mom, look at those people. Yuck!"

"Mommy, what are they doing?"

"It's nothing, kids. They're just saying hello. Come along. Let's get to the beach." Molly turned a bright shade of red, but the mother just winked at them.

"Oh, Nate, I'm humiliated. What must she think of us?"

Nate took her hand as they slowly began to walk towards the beach. "She wishes she was young again, madly in love with her man, and not saddled down with kids."

"Is that want you think of kids, that they saddle you down?"

"No, that's not what I meant. I --"

Nate tried to explain himself, but only seemed to get into deeper trouble.

"Because I want children someday, don't you?"

"Sure, but when the time is right, and I'm with the right person."

Molly was quiet for a moment. She kicked at a stone. "Am I the right person?"

Nate hesitated to say what was in his heart. He was afraid of scaring her off, but if he didn't speak his mind he might lose her. "You have been since the moment I laid eyes on you," he whispered. "You are my one and only 'right' person."

She studied his eyes, looking deeply into the color changes of his irises. It was a place a girl could get lost. What was he saying? She was too young for anything serious. Isn't that what her mother had been warning her about? "Nate, I, uh, I, let's talk about this when we're in a more private setting." Molly suddenly changed moods and yelled, "To the beach," and ran away from him.

'Did I just blow it?' Nate asked himself. Then he ran after her across the hot sand, and they jumped into the cool refreshing water, squealing and splashing each other like little children.

Chapter Five

A few weeks later, Nate and Molly took some time to be alone after dinner on a bright Sunday afternoon. "Tell me about yourself, Nate. I mean really tell me things I don't know." Molly spread their picnic blanket on the banks of the stream that ran through the Sparks' property, several acres away from the house. The thick growth of Frazier pines totally blocked them out from all activity. The two felt as if they were on an island all alone. The only sounds were coming from a lone chain saw off in the distance. Molly was returning to college tomorrow and even though she wasn't that far from home, once she became immersed in her studies and the various school activities, she would not come home often.

"I think you know it all. I haven't held anything back."

As Molly opened the containers of snacks and popped the lid of a couple of cans of Coke, she watched him closely. Nate had his back to her now as he tossed pebbles in the water. The soft plopping sound helped to fill the space which was void of words as he made a decision about going further in revealing his past. He turned to look at her, and then moved to sit on the blanket, but even then he sat so he could look at the water and not at her face.

Nate cleared his throat, took a deep breath, and began to bare his soul. If he could trust anyone, he knew it was Molly. "It's not a pretty picture, so I never talk about it. My childhood was nothing like yours, at all, as you know. But what I haven't told you is that my parents fought all the time, my father drank too much, and later cheated on my mom, and that led to my mother drinking. Neither one seemed to notice that I existed. I made my own breakfast and packed my own lunch every day, then got myself to school. No one ever came to a parent-teacher conference or showed up for a school play. In a nutshell, they really didn't want me.

"Poor Nate, how did you handle it all?"

"You see, that's one of the reasons I don't talk about it. Please don't say 'poor Nate.'"

"I'm sorry, I didn't mean --"

"I know, it's just that I've come to realize that we are all given different crosses to bear in life, and being left alone at a firehouse was mine. It shaped the rest of my life, but I won't let it define me. I am not my adopted parents, and I have no idea of my real heritage, so I have to be my own person."

"What about after you finish school? What will you do then?"

"I'm not sure, but I think I took the wrong turn with accounting. I have to figure it out soon. I really enjoy growing and pruning these trees. The accounting will come in handy if I decide to run my own farm someday. But one thing I know for sure is that I really want a home of my own, and a family – children, lots of kids. And a Christmas tree with colored lights – none of those small twinkly white ones. And presents, lots and lots of presents for everyone. And I will never miss a birthday of one of my children for as long as they live. I will always be there for ballgames, and I will be the loudest clapper at school plays." Molly noticed that he brushed away a tear, and her heart ached for him.

She was quiet for a few seconds, then she placed her hand on his arm, and said softly, "Do you have anyone in mind you want to take with you on this life journey?"

When Nate felt the warmth of her hand, and heard the question she was asking, he stopped breathing. He turned to look at her now, compassion and love was like an electrical charge flowing from her directly to him.

"You must know by now that I love you, Molly. I have from the moment I first met you, and then later when you threw a pinecone at my back, it sealed the deal for me." He tried a teasing smile. They looked at each for what seemed an eternity, then he moved to kiss her, but found they were in an awkward position. He wasn't sure if he was the one or if Molly was the one who first made the move to lie down on their blanket. It happened slowly, their lips joining on the way down. Nate's body formed to hers, and she allowed it. In fact, she seemed to want it as much as he did.

"I love you, Molly. I love you so much it hurts," he whispered. His hands began to roam, and he slowly moved on top of her.

Molly moaned softly, and began to respond to his caresses, but suddenly she heard her mother's voice in her head. She sat up abruptly, startling Nate, and embarrassing him at the same time. "Nate, I can't." Tears filled her eyes. "Please, don't think badly of me. I'm just not ready."

"Oh, Molly, honey. It's all my fault. I'm so sorry. I just love you so much, and I let things go too far." He pulled her to him once more, aching for more than she was ready to give, but he said, "Please forgive me."

Molly's mind was racing. She wanted to give him what he wanted, but she knew it would change the course of her life. If she found herself pregnant, she could be in the same position as Nate's biological mother, and the cycle would repeat itself. Besides all of that, she would not allow herself to become a tree farmer's wife. "Of course, let's just take it slow, okay?" She smiled sweetly and then changed the direction of the conversation, by saying, "For now, let's eat."

It had not gone unnoticed by Nate that Molly had not returned his declaration of love, and it was difficult to pretend that he was not hurt, but he had covered his feelings plenty of times, so he was sure Molly never knew his pain. He would be patient for as long as it took. He would slowly, over time, convince her to love him back. She was the only one he wanted – the only one he would ever want.

≈

The next day, Nate found Molly in front of the farmhouse, loading her car. He knew that soon the rest of the family would come outside, so he took this opportunity while they were alone to pull her into his arms. He breathed a sigh of relief when she accepted his kisses eagerly.

"I'm going to miss you so much," he sighed into her hair. "Will you call often? I have a real cell phone now with a good provider, so I can talk longer."

"Of course, I'll call. Being away from you will be torture." And the moment she said it, she knew she meant it. She had been such a fool. She loved Nate, but she didn't know what was holding her back from saying it out loud. "I'll think of you every day, and when I come back for Thanksgiving, we'll spend lots of time together." Molly pulled Nate back to her, and kissed him passionately, pressing her body into his.

Relief spread through Nate. She really did love him; he could tell. It would just take time for her to say it. She was still young, yet, after all, he thought. It didn't matter that they were the same age. Nate had lived a far different life than Molly had, and he had not been protected and pampered. Molly still had a lot of growing up to do. After hugging her parents and brother goodbye, Molly drove off, and headed down the road to pick up Claire. Nate was already looking forward to their first talk on his new cell phone. He wanted to hear all about her days on the big college campus.

But Nate was disappointed when he did not hear from Molly as often as he thought he would. Most of the time he had to call her, and then she was usually off to a class or lecture. It was most disturbing when she told him she was going out with the gang for pizza and drinks. It wasn't that he thought she would cheat on him, he trusted her 100 percent, but he felt left out of her life. Who were these new friends she had, and what did they do together? November could not come soon enough for him.

The tree farm was entering into what they called the pressure cooker days as Christmas was just a few months around the corner. Cora took orders from their wholesalers and arranged for delivery dates, while the men finalized the pruning, cleaning the barn to get ready for retail customers, and made sure the baler was functioning properly. The closer they got to Thanksgiving, the bigger the push to succeed and make money while they had the chance.

Most of the men who had been on the farm when Nate first started, had left. The turnover rate was high, so he was now senior in the field, next to Freddy. He did his work efficiently and without complaint. And, best of all, the Sunday dinners continued. For the first time in his life, Nate had a real family.

≈

The air was crisp, cool, and very still. The smell of pine smoke was in the air as the last of the trimmed branches were thrown on the brush fire. Molly could see the spiral of smoke rising up to the clear blue sky as she pulled in the driveway of her family home. And just as she expected, Nate was waiting for her on the porch. She had texted ahead to announce that she was near the farm after dropping Claire off, where Freddy was anxiously waiting there to meet her best friend and the woman he was in love with. Claire talked about nothing and no one but Freddy all the time. For Molly it was annoying hearing about how fabulous her brother was. Yes, he was a good guy, and all, but Molly had wanted to experience life a little at college. She wanted to forget about farm life and the little town she came from. She did not want to be reminded of home every single minute. Sometimes she had wished Claire had not been her roommate. Her friend could be a real stick in the mud. But that was all behind her now for at least the next five days. She did not have to be back to class until Wednesday of next week. And she didn't want to think about classes and studying. And there was Nate, waiting on the porch with a big grin, looking so good. He might be one of the handsomest boys she had ever known, and he was all hers. She did love him. She had had to admit that to herself, especially on those lonely nights, when she found herself alone in her room with no one to talk to. But Molly was still spreading her wings, and she was afraid to commit to anyone.

Cora and Duane had tactfully waited inside the house so the young people could have a few moments alone together. Molly was sure they were looking out the window, but she didn't care. She bounced out of the car and flew into Nate's arms. He was thrilled with the greeting. He kissed her as he twirled her around, and the sensation of flying was exhilarating. His lips tasted so good. Molly had little butterflies and tingles throughout her whole body. She kissed him back and wished he would never let go. 'What's happening to me?' she wondered. Then she said out loud, "I missed you so much, Nate. More than I could have ever imagined."

"Oh Molly, Molly, my sweet, I missed you, too."

When he finally set her down, Molly saw tears in Nate's eyes. She felt guilty for not thinking about him as often as she should have while she was gone. She really did love being with him. He knew her better than anyone else on Earth. She buried her face into his chest, and sighed. He was warm and comfortable. She knew at that moment, that she loved him, truly loved him. When she looked up at him, she, too, had tears in her eyes.

That Thanksgiving was everything Nate had ever dreamed it would be. He really felt a part of the family, now. He helped in the kitchen for a few minutes, just so he could be near Molly more, but then he heard his name being called by the men so he joined Duane and Freddy to watch the Detroit Lions play the Chicago Bears. As soon as the game was over, everyone jumped up and yelled, 'Let's eat.' The smells from the kitchen had been wafting into the living room for quite a while and their stomachs were growling with anticipation. Cora was a wonderful cook. She served a traditional meal with roasted turkey, stuffing, mashed potatoes, and gravy, followed by pumpkin and apple pies for dessert. Nate couldn't wipe the grin off his face, especially when Molly asked if he wanted to take a walk after the dishes were cleared and washed. At that moment he knew this was the best life could offer.

Molly reached out to take Nate's hand as they walked back towards their favorite spot by the creek. They swung their arms back and forth like children, laughing the whole time. It was a beautiful day and Nate knew this would be the perfect time to bring up their future. Molly still had not said the 'I love you' words, but he was sure it would come soon.

Once they arrived at the water's edge, Molly suddenly became serious. "Nate, I have something to talk to you about."

"I do, too," said Nate excitedly. "Who goes first?"

Molly bit her lip. Nate seemed to be bursting with something he had to say. "You go first. You look like you are going to come unglued if you don't get it out."

"Okay, I will." Nate took a deep breath, about to say what he had been waiting to say all day, what he had practiced in front of the mirror. But with one look into her beautiful eyes, he felt as though he was falling into an abyss. He was hopelessly in love. He kissed Molly with more passion than she had ever felt from him. It literally took her breath away, but she knew she must be strong, because what she had to say, might change his devotion to her forever.

Nate cleared his throat and smiling with excitement, placed one hand on her cheek. "My sweet, my love, my Molly. I have been thinking about us for a very long time. I know you are the only girl for me. I would go to the ends of the Earth to protect you and care for you. I also know that we are still very young and you have college to finish – well, so do I actually, but maybe not so many years. But what I guess I am trying to say is that I would like to ask you if you will marry me someday. I just feel like we are ready for a commitment. You know, so we can have a long range plan for the future. I'm head over heels in love with you. What do you say? Will you have me as a future husband? Will you marry me someday?" Nate saw the shocked look on her face, and felt he had to continue. "Oh, I didn't mean this as a formal proposal of marriage, yet. When the time is right, I'll do it properly. I'm sorry, I didn't mean to scare you."

Molly felt as if she couldn't breathe. It was a suffocating feeling, as if it were choking the life out of her. But when she finally got her voice, she simply said, "Oh, Nate. Oh, Nate. Oh, oh." A single tear slip down her cheek.

"What is it, Molly?"

"Before I answer that question, I need to tell you my news. I have been faking it about school at MSU. I've been miserable. I really don't like being at a big college. It's overwhelming, and most of the kids just want to party all the time. Studying and learning is on their backburner. And it's a huge expense. I know Mom and Dad are struggling to put me through, even with my grants, loans, and the savings I worked so many years on this farm to accumulate. It's just not working. I've decided to transfer next year to a small teaching college in Iowa."

"Iowa? But that's so far away."

"I know. I haven't told them about it yet. I wanted to talk to you first. It means I won't be coming home so often. Maybe not for Thanksgiving, but I would still be here for Christmas, and most likely over spring break, and of course, all summer long."

"Yes, I guess I understand. It'll be tough, but we can manage. Other people have done it, right? All long distance romances aren't doomed. I'm disappointed, but I get it. You have to do what is right for you. When will you go?"

"Not until next year, so we still have Christmas break, spring break, and all summer to be together."

"Well, what about my proposal? You haven't answered."

Molly hesitated, but it must be said. "I do like you more than any boy I have ever known. And my parents and brother are crazy about you."

Nate could hear the 'but' coming, and he began to quake with fear. "But," he prompted.

"But, I'm not sure if I'm in love. I mean, I love you, I'm sure of that, but maybe not in the right way, yet. Don't look so downtrodden. You are the *only* boy I want to be with. No one else interests me at all." She stroked his cheek, then laid her head on his chest. "I don't want to hurt you, Nate. I just want to be honest. I'm just not ready to think about marriage, that's all."

"Okay, maybe I *was* pushing too soon, but now I'm afraid when you go away, you'll forget about me."

"It's not going to happen – ever. You will always be my pinecone man." She poked his chest and giggled, hoping to put him in a better mood, but it was too late. His fear had already caused his blood to run cold.

They made a pact that they would not talk about her moving away to another state until next fall when the time came for her to actually leave. They would go on as always and enjoy the rest of this holiday season and spend every minute of Christmas together and then the entire summer. But all Nate could see was long lonely months without her. He was already dreading Wednesday when she would leave him again. That night, he marked on his calendar the day she would be home for Christmas. It was only a month away, and she was still here. He ached for the time when he could hold her all night long. His desires were growing stronger, and it became painful for him to think of ever losing her. He would convince her they were meant to be. He prayed every night that she would feel the love as strongly as he did, and when he finally fell asleep, it was to dreams of her sweet lips and soft sighs.

Chapter Six

"Merry Christmas, everyone," called Freddy as he hauled in the best blue spruce he could find on the property.

"Look at that. It's a beaut. But, hey," laughed his father, "you're supposed to save the best for the customers. This one is too perfect. Someone was on their game when they were pruning her."

"Yeah, she *is* perfect, isn't she?" The men had a habit of referring to the trees as females. Possibly because the pinecones represented new life. "I hope you don't mind. I wanted this Christmas to be special."

"Is there something we should know about?" asked Duane, now curious as to why Freddy wanted to put in extra effort, when he usually had his fill of Christmas trees at this time of year.

"You'll know soon enough. I'll make an announcement when we're all together. And also with it being Nate's first Christmas with us, I wanted it to be very meaningful for him. I know he didn't have a good childhood, so I thought maybe we could change his mind about the holiday he usually dreads."

"You're right, son. We need to do everything we can to show him what a real Christmas is like with a loving family. He's a wonderful young man. I'd like to be the best example possible for him."

"Yeah, me too. Well, I'll get to it, if you just help me place it in the stand and make sure she's straight."

"Hmm, I'll never get tired of the smell of pine," said Cora, as she walked into the room to find her two favorite men hard at work. "Freddy, it looks like you've outdone yourself this year. Look at that. A perfect conical shape all the way around, and the height is just right." Cora looked at her son's face. He was beaming from ear to ear. Something was up. She hadn't seen him this excited since he was a boy opening presents on Christmas morning. "Does anyone know if Nate is coming over?"

"No, I haven't seen him in a while," said Duane. "I assumed he'd be here, already."

"Well, did anyone invite him?" she asked with her hands on her hips.

"I didn't," said Freddy. "You, pop?"

"No, me either."

"Well for Pete's sake. You guys are terrible. We don't want to leave that poor kid out there in the shanty all alone, while we're in here decorating. Freddy go get him, or call his phone." She walked away clicking her tongue. "Where are your manners?" she muttered. "I raised you better than that -- both of you," she yelled over her shoulder.

≈

Nate was in the bunkhouse alone. His two roommates had gone out to get something to eat and to look for girls, and even though he was asked to go along, he turned them down. Looking for girls was the last thing on his mind. Molly was coming home tomorrow and other than Christmas with her family, he should be able to see her every day for a week. He sat on the edge of his bed, knife and piece of wood in his hand, carving into the soft wood as the shavings fell to the floor. He had agonized over what he could get her for Christmas. It had to be something special but not expensive. And he wanted it to be meaningful. Molly was a very creative person; she loved crafts and homemade items. Nate had never thought of himself in that way, but he decided to try his hand at carving. If it didn't turn out well, he wouldn't tell her about it and she would never know of his failure, but much to his own surprise, he seemed to have a hidden talent for carving. At the moment he was working on the third in a set of small pinecones, each one a different size. The pinecones were meaningful to him, and he hoped it would be the same for her. They represented the farm itself, but most of all the first time they had talked and spent some time together. That day when she had pitched a small pinecone at his back was one he would never forget. When he turned around to see that unruly, curly hair poking out of her stocking cap, and her big light grey eyes laughing at him, he fell in love at that moment. He knew people would say it was crazy, but that's the way it was. He had been attracted to her when they were first introduced, but love hit him like a lightning bolt on that day in the pines.

Nate was startled out of his reverie, with a knock on the door, followed by Freddy calling, "Hurry up, you dope, it's cold out here."

Nate tucked his latest creation under his pillow and kicked the shavings under the bed. "I'm coming." As he opened the door Freddy stepped in, bringing a swirl of snow with him.

"Man, it's getting bad out there. Are you coming to the house?"

"Why? What's going on?"

"We're setting up the tree and putting up some decorations. Mom expected you to be there."

"Oh, I didn't know. Don't you wait for Molly?"

"Usually we do, but this year we thought we'd get a head start on the decorations and wait to finish the tree when she arrives. Mom, said we got a late start because of the way the holiday falls. With Christmas on a Sunday, it's thrown our schedule off."

"Yeah, we sure have been busy." Grabbing his coat and slipping into his boots, Nate continued, "What's the schedule for next week?"

"We'll have to work on Christmas Eve. We always do. Lots of people like to get their trees then; it seems terribly late to me, but if that's their tradition we try to stay open for them. But we only work until 7; then it'll be family time. And of course, we're closed on Christmas Day."

Nate locked the door behind them, and they began the walk to the main house, boots squeaking in the fresh wet snow. "Do you go to Christmas Eve services?" asked Nate.

"Mom wouldn't let us miss it. It's a candlelight service, so very pretty and meaningful. We softly sing Christmas carols, as we wait for the birth of the baby Jesus."

"I'm looking forward to it. I've never done anything like that before."

"Well, here we are, make sure you knock all of the snow off of your boots."

Nate laughed, "I know the drill. Wouldn't want Mrs. S upset with me."

The tree was in its place, naked as a jaybird, as the saying goes, but beautiful all the same. Nate had never been in a home with a Christmas tree that large before. As far as he was concerned no decorations were needed. It was spectacular in its own right. He shyly ducked his head, "Thanks for asking me over, Mrs. Sparks."

"Now, what did I tell you? Cora is just fine. Don't just stand there, grab a box and start stringing lights over the mantle and archways."

Cora put on some Christmas music and they all sang as they worked. Nate had to pinch himself to make sure this was all real. 'People really did these things? It doesn't just happen in the movies?' he thought.

"Now, I know you guys will be hard at work tomorrow, but Nate, when Molly comes home, you take off for a few hours to be with her. I know she's looking forward to seeing you."

"Thank you, Mrs. – Cora. That would be great." He grinned and went back to his task at hand, promising to make the house the best Molly had ever seen.

When Molly arrived, in a swirl of snow and wind, she brought with her the excitement of being out of school for two weeks, the joy of being home with family, and the thrill of seeing Nate. Nate grabbed her on the front porch before the rest of the family even knew she was there. They stole a few moments to themselves for kisses, kisses that curled Molly's toes, and surprised her with unexpected passion. She was most surprised at how much she had missed Nate. If it wasn't for her family waiting inside for her, she would have suggested they go off by themselves, where they could share some more private time.

"Oh, Nate, I missed you so much."

"Molly, Molly, I can't believe you're here. Umm, you smell so good, you taste so good. I can't get enough of you." Nate's hands began to roam over her body, but with the downy jacket, and long heavy scarf, he was not getting what he really wanted.

"Whoa, cowboy, my parents are on the other side of that door."

"You're right, I'm sorry, I should never put you in an embarrassing situation. I love you, Molly, I just simply love you."

Molly looked at him with those huge grey eyes, but all she could get out was, "I know, Nate. Now, let's go in. It's freezing out here. Oh – but first, help me get my gifts and suitcase out of the car."

The two young people came in the door, overloaded with shopping bags and suitcases. If these were all Christmas gifts, Nate realized he had a lot of shopping to do yet. He had never seen anything like it, and these were only the items Molly was giving. He could tell this promised to be the best Christmas he had ever had!

"Here she is," exclaimed Cora.

Duane jumped up to help with the bags. "Wow! It looks like Santa has arrived early. Mmm, what's in this one?"

"Dad! Most of them aren't wrapped yet. Mom, make him stop."

"Okay, okay, I'll wait until Christmas, but you know me. Hide them well, because I might snoop."

"Oh, Dad. That's more Freddy's problem. Remember that time -- "

"Hey, did I hear my name?" piped in Freddy. "And by the way, I never snooped."

"Come on, Freddy. You always knew what you were getting before you unwrapped the gifts."

"Well, now that I'm older, I'll admit to it," confessed her brother, "I might have looked at a few, but I soon learned that it wasn't fun anymore, and I gave up my detective work after that."

"Well, frankly," said Molly, "I don't trust any of you, except for Nate, of course."

Nate laughed. He loved being a part of this family. "That's only because you don't know me well enough, yet. This will be our first Christmas together. How do you know what I'm like?"

Molly's eyes got big. "You mean you would spoil it for me, knowing how I love to give presents?"

"Just teasing. Remember I don't have a reference point for this discussion. It's all new to me."

There was silence for a moment as the family took in what he had said. Here he was, a nineteen-year-old young man, and he had never experienced the joy of Christmas giving.

89

"Well, we are about to take care of that. You will celebrate with us. I expect you here, bright and early, on Christmas morning. Now, let's get Molly's things upstairs, and get back to decorating. There's a lot of baking to do yet, and I have to figure out how to get it all in, while helping customers with their trees and wreaths. Are we ready for long days and nights?"

They grouped in a huddle with their hands touching, then said "One, two, three, CHRISTMAS!"

"Hey, Mom, can I cut out for a few? I want to see Claire."

"Sure, just be careful. It's snowing hard right now. Take your time. She'll be waiting for you when you get there, I'm sure." His mother winked. Knowing that her two children were both in love with such wonderful people, warmed her heart.

"Deck the halls with boughs of holly," sang Molly.

"Fa la la la la, la la la la," added Nate.

≈

The next few days flew by with a flurry of activity. The boys drove the four wheelers through the rows of trees, as customers called out to them that they had found their tree. Then a quick cut with the chain saw, or if the customers preferred they could cut it manually with a hack saw. Some of the customers enjoyed lifting the tree onto the four wheeler themselves, some let their children take part in the process. Then they would take the long walk back to the barn where their tree was waiting for them, as Duane had already done his magic with the tree wrapper. The young men would lift the tree to the top of the car or place it in the back of an SUV or pickup truck. All the while people were laughing and teasing and calling Merry Christmas when they left.

Molly and Nate barely saw each other during the rush hours. She was busy selling the wreaths and serving hot cocoa, while her mother stood at the cash register in front of a space heater. It was an exhausting business, but during this particular week before Christmas, well worth it. The Christmas spirit could be felt with each new person that pulled into their driveway, and only rarely did someone get on their nerves. Usually, it was a man who felt like it had taken time out of his business day to get a tree for his kids. Nate related to a family like this, and tried to connect with the kids in some special way, by teasing them about Santa, or asking what they wanted for Christmas. His kindness didn't go unnoticed by both Molly and Cora.

Finally, on Christmas Eve, they turned off the lights at 7:00 p.m. when it was obvious there were no more people coming. Exhausted, feet aching, backs hurting, they sat by the heater in the barn for a few moments, sharing some of the hot cocoa.

"Wow, that was crazy," said Freddy.

"Yeah, you can tell the farm is aging. We had so many more trees to sell this year, and way more customers," added Molly.

"And when you figure in the wholesale business," said Duane, "I'd say we did all right. I'm happy; how about you guys?"

The entire family nodded. "And we want to thank all of our help for doing such a great job. You kept your enthusiasm, and we worked together like a well-oiled machine."

"If it's all right, I'd like to head out now to visit with my family," said Rafael, one of the new hires.

"I really enjoyed it, Mr. Sparks," said Bob. "I'm going to see my family tomorrow, so I'll just head back to the bunkhouse and get some rest. I have a long drive ahead of me."

"Sure, both of you guys are free to go. We won't be back to work for a month now, then it will be time to work on farm equipment in a well-heated barn. Thanks again for everything. Your checks and bonuses are by the cash register. Cora, can you get those?"

As Nate stood to go, also, Molly said, "Are you going to the candlelight service with us, Nate?"

"I'd love to. What time are you leaving?"

"About 9:30. Candlelight service starts at 10:00."

"Okay, great. That will give me time to shower and get presentable again. I have pine pitch all over me."

"In that case, I won't hug you goodbye," laughed Molly. "You know what I think about pine pitch."

On the way out, Nate picked up his check and was surprised to see a substantial bonus check included. It would make a nice dent in his college tuition payment which was due on the first of the year.

The church service was the most special service Nate had ever been to. It was quiet and reverent, and the candles they each held in their hands added an extra glow of holiness. The best part was being with the family and holding Molly's hand through the singing of "Silent Night." Nate was filled with the wonderful awesomeness of Jesus and Christmas all the way to the depths of his soul.

Chapter Seven

The phone by his bed was making an irritating ringing noise. Nate struggled to reach it, dropped it, than managed to open his eyes up enough to answer the call.

"Molly? What's wrong?"

"Nate! Santa has come. It's Christmas! Where are you?"

"Wh – What?" His blurry eyes tried to focus on the clock. "But it's only 6:00."

"Yes, that's the time we unwrap presents, then we'll have a big farmhouse breakfast."

"Oh, sorry, I thought since you were all adults, you slept in a little."

"No, silly, we believe in always nurturing the child within. Come on, it's fun. Now, get to it. We're all waiting."

"Okay, I'll be there in a sec."

"Don't bother getting dressed. Come in your pajamas. It's tradition."

Nate hopped out of bed and glanced down at his t shirt and boxers. That wouldn't do, so he pulled on pair of sweat pants and a U of M sweat shirt. He grabbed his slippers, pulled on his boots, and tugged on his coat, not bothering to zip it up. He went out the door, but only took two steps before he realized he had forgotten something very important, so he went back in and grabbed the large shopping bag filled with wrapped presents for the family, and one very special one for Molly. Then he hopped on the four-wheeler and buzzed up to the house in record time.

"He's here! He's here," yelled Molly. "Merry Christmas, Nate." She kissed him longingly, right there in the foyer, with family just around the corner. She tugged off his jacket, and laughed at his attire. "That's what you call pj's? Well, at least you wore the right colors. Can't go wrong with Maize and Blue."

"It's a whole lot better than what I was wearing to sleep in, believe me. Maybe someday you'll get to see it for yourself."

Molly blushed. "Nate, shh, they're coming."

"Merry Christmas," yelled Duane. "Come on, let's get this show on the road!"

"Oh, Dad, you just want to get it over with so you can eat," said Freddy, as he slapped Nate on the back. "Come on, Dude. Let's go. Molly is fierce when it comes to opening presents. You're about to see another side of her."

As Nate rounded the corner, his first view of the living room made him gasp out loud. The tree was lit and seemed to be glowing from a heavenly source. Candles on the mantle were burning, emitting a scented mixture of cinnamon and vanilla, and combined with the scent of pine from the tree, it made him light-headed with joy. But the best of all, were the gifts under the tree. Nate had never been interested in receiving gifts necessarily, but the idea of the whole family experience enticed him. Gifts of all shapes and sizes were stacked under the lowest branches. Some had colorful bows and others were topped with bells or pinecones. It looked to all the world to him like a fairytale -- something he had only viewed on TV or in his dreams as a child, something he had always hoped for on Christmas morning, but never, ever took part in. The Sparks family knew this would be a special moment for Nate, and they were excited to share it with him, but when they saw the look on his face, each person present had tears in their eyes.

Nate felt ridiculous, when the only word he could squeak out was, "Wow!"

Molly was the first to take his elbow and move him forward into the room. Then her mother recovered and said, "We're so glad you could be with us this morning. Merry Christmas, dear. Now, come over here and sit down." She patted the couch cushion, while she took an easy chair. Molly sat next to Nate, and Freddy dropped to the floor. "I guess I'm Santa this morning. Sit Dad, let's get this show on the road, as you like to say."

Nate watched in awe as each person opened their gifts, thanking the gift-giver with loving respect. Molly gave him a trapper hat with a fur brim and earflaps, and a book by his favorite author. When he placed his hat on his head, Molly's Dad and brother laughed, saying he looked like he was ready to shoot a bear. Cora said he looked cute, and she was sure it would keep him very warm. He loved it because it came from Molly. Anything she gave him would have been perfect in his eyes.

When it was time for the family to open gifts from him, he was so nervous his heart was racing. He had spent an afternoon in the city shopping for just the perfect items: a soft colorful scarf for Cora, a pair of leather gloves for Duane, and the latest vinyl album by Freddy's favorite band. But for Molly he had something special. He had put his heart and soul into his work.

Freddy held the small box out to her, and said, "Molly, this one is from Nate."

She hesitated for a moment, looking at him, hoping it would not be anything too personal that might embarrass her. She pulled at the ribbon and carefully tore off the paper.

"Hey, that's not your style at all," said Freddy. "Get to it, girl."

When she lifted the lid of the box, she discovered three wooden pinecones, of various sizes. She could tell they were handcrafted. "Oh, Nate, these are beautiful." Looking into his eyes, she was the only one who knew of their significance – of the love he was expressing. "Did you – did you carve these yourself?"

Nate nodded modestly. "I hope they're okay. It was my first try."

Molly handed the box to her mother so she could get a closer look. "My goodness," said Cora, "you have talent. You should make more items like this. They're beautiful."

The praise made Nate's face turn a bright shade of red. He had never known that families like this were real. They were kind and generous and loving. He made a vow to himself that for the rest of his life he would try to follow in their footsteps. And he prayed that, with Molly, he would be a part of their lives forever.

"That was the last gift," said Duane, clapping his hands. "Let's eat. I'm starving."

"Dad, you're always starving."

"That's because your Mom is such a great cook. Let's go! Time for breakfast."

It was the best Christmas and the worst Christmas. And Nate had had many more bad Christmases than good. It was the best because of the family, the gift giving, the church service, and Molly.

His love for her continued to grow, even though he had no idea how he could love her more each day. Freddy left after breakfast to spend time with Claire's family. Everyone knew a marriage proposal was coming soon and suspected it might be today.

Nate and Molly cuddled side by side next to the fireplace and talked about everything and anything. They never ran out of topics to discuss. Molly's mom was in the kitchen preparing for a big Christmas dinner, where she preferred to be alone, listening to Handel's Messiah as she cooked. Molly's dad had gone out to the barn to feed the chickens and geese. Animals did not take a break for the holidays. Molly suspected he enjoyed the quiet as he seemed to take extra time out there puttering about.

Nate looked around and when he knew they were alone for sure, he pulled Molly in, and began kissing her the way he had wanted to all day. Molly was more than happy to return his passion, but she pulled away sooner than he would have liked. Breathing heavily, she said, "Nate, my family is here."

"No one is watching," he whispered, and pulled her back, seeking her lips again.

"Nate, no. That's enough."

"Okay, I'm sorry, Molly. It's just that I'm over the moon in love with you. I can't seem to control myself," he chuckled, quite embarrassed with his behavior.

"Yes," laughed Molly, "so you've told me before. But remember we're going to take it slow. Right?"

"Right, right. I promise."

They spent every spare moment of the rest of the holiday together. Whenever they were alone, Nate would profess his love, always waiting for Molly to return those waited for words. If only she would say I love you in the way he wanted to hear it, he would be a happy man. But Molly held back, not knowing for sure what was stopping her. She did love Nate, she knew that was true, and her sexual desire was definitely present, but with so little experience, she wasn't sure if it was the kind of love that would last a lifetime. She wanted the same thing her parents had, but she wanted no part of farm living, and in her mind, the two went together. And now , more and more, it looked like Nate was leaning towards the tree farming business himself.

The night before Molly returned to school, Nate told her how much he would miss her, but this time he held back from declarations of love other than to say quietly 'I love you,' when they parted. Molly simply said, "I know," and kissed him softly. As she drove away, Nate had a dreadful feeling that he would lose her. And as the days passed, he feared that he was right. The phone calls were less frequent this time. She was chatty about her daily activities more than talking about anything personal. And worst of all, she did not come home for spring break, but decided to go to Florida with friends instead. When Molly came home for the summer, she seemed like a different person. She still looked like the beautiful girl he had fallen in love with, maybe more so, but the connection between them seemed to have been lost.

Sitting on his bunkbed, Nate pondered what was going wrong. He was good looking – he knew that because he had been told so all of his life. Girls quite often flirted with him. He always tried to be kind and generous, and he was a good worker. He was a people pleaser, so people just plain liked him. But Molly was different. Yes, she liked him. And she seemed to enjoy being with him. They spent many days, boating, swimming, and walking trails. They went bowling, drove go karts, and even played laser tag one time. On those days, Nate was the happiest he had ever been in his life, so at summer's end, when Molly had to pack to go to Iowa to her new college, Nate decided it was now or never.

The autumn moon was huge, shining a beacon down on them, as they waited for the hidden stars to show themselves. Nate and Molly sat in the yard swing holding hands, quietly moving back and forth. The crickets and tree frogs called loudly to each other, blending their voices into one huge symphony. The rhythm and sounds had mellowed Molly into a peace she had not felt in a long time; she placed her head on Nate's shoulder.

"I can't stand it any longer, Molly. You know how I feel. You've always known," said Nate. "I need to say it out loud once more, or I will burst."

"Nate -- I"

"Shh," he said, as he placed two fingers on her lips. "Let me finish. You're going away even further from me, now." He paused and looked into her eyes to see if this was too much for her, but it didn't matter what she thought anymore. He had to go on. When she didn't try to stop him, he proceeded. "I love you so much. I want to spend the rest of our lives *together*. I want to be the father of your children. I know we're young. I just turned twenty this summer, and you will, too, in another month, but I need to know before you leave, if you will commit to me and me only. We're so good together. I don't want to share you with anyone else."

Molly knew this was the turning point. She did not want to hurt Nate, but she still was not sure of her feelings. One day she was madly in love and the next day she saw a cute guy and her head was turned. She began once again with, "Nate, I -- " but when she saw tears form in his eyes about to spill over, she could not break his heart. "Yes, Nate, I'll wait for you. I'm committing to you, I promise." she said surprising herself. And at that moment she discovered that she really meant it. "When I graduate we can talk about marriage then. I do love you. I really do. You are my pinecone man, after all."

Nate pulled her to him, and swallowed hard on order to stifle the sob that was about to erupt, so that only quiet tears rolled into her hair. She would be his. She would wait. She had promised. It was all he needed to hear.

The suitcase was finally packed and loaded, her backpack was overstuffed, and she still had books, bedding, and her computer to jam into the car. Molly was glad her father had agreed to drive her to the campus in Iowa. Her mother had wanted to go, too, but someone had to stay near the farm to keep things moving. Even though it was late August, they were beginning the push toward Christmas already.

Saying goodbye to Nate had been difficult last night. In the light of day, she realized she might have given Nate false hope. School would be strange and new and exciting. Molly had no idea what was to come, and even though she did love Nate, she was a realist, and she knew life was uncertain. Her next trip home would be Thanksgiving, by then she had promised herself to stop waffling and make up her mind about Nate once and for all. He had a right to be sure of his future.

Their kiss by the car was short and sweet since other family members were present. Molly whispered in his ear, "Goodbye, pinecone man."

"Goodbye, sweetheart. Did you remember to take the pinecones I made you?"

"Yes, silly, they're in my bag already."

"Good. They'll remind you of who you are, and bring you back to me."

College was everything she had hoped for. A smaller campus gave her the opportunity to feel like she belonged to something. She no longer felt lost in the crowd. Molly made friends easily and often went to her roommate's house for the weekend. Her family lived a short distance away. She was much more social in Iowa; she attended parties, joined discussion groups, and began to work on the school paper. Often when Nate called, she was too busy to talk, or she was just on her way out the door. And when she tried to return his call, she would catch him working in the field. Promises were made to call later in the day when they could talk, but while Nate waited anxiously for her to be free, she sometimes completely forgot about him, and days would go by before they were able to connect other than a quick text.

As Thanksgiving neared, a new friend who was from Colorado, asked her to go home with her so they could go skiing at a lodge near her house. The invitation was too good to turn down, and Molly eagerly accepted.

Nate was disappointed, but said he understood and would see her at Christmas.

But that Colorado trip changed everything. That's when Molly met Chad Clairmont. He was tall, blond, extremely good looking, very athletic, and very rich, and for reasons Molly had never understood, he was attracted to a Michigan farm girl. As soon as he set his sights on her, Molly's head was turned, and before long, they were skiing down the slopes together, enjoying hot chocolate by the fireplace, and talking into the wee hours about books, music, and life goals.

Chad was already out of college and had begun his career working in his father's boating business in Minnesota. He was only in Colorado for a short ski trip. He had intended to flirt a little and go on his way, but after only a few days of being together, the two already had formed a strong attachment. Molly realized later that when she was with Chad, she had never once thought about Nate.

Molly and Chad parted at the ended of the week, but promised to text, talk, and use Skype or Facetime on their iPhones. And they had, every single day, and sometimes more than that. Molly was head over heels in love. Chad was head over heels with the idea of love.

As time came for her to go home for Christmas, Molly began to worry about facing Nate. She didn't want to hurt his feelings, but it had to be done. At this point he had no idea that she would be breaking up with him over winter break. It was going to be difficult in more ways than one, because she knew her parents and Freddy would not be pleased, either. She decided to make the best of it, and not say anything until it was time to leave again.

Chapter Eight

It was the second best Christmas in his entire life. Nate would never forget last year, but this Christmas came in at the top of his list of best holidays ever. A big snow front came in early in the day on Christmas Eve, so the family decided it was best not to attend the candlelight service this year. The plows were doing everything they could to keep up, but the roads were still too dangerous. They played games, drank hot chocolate, and snacked on the many beautiful Christmas cookies placed artfully on a tray. Cora had made several dips for crackers and chips, and there was also a large tray of cheese and deli meats. At the end of the evening they said their goodnights to Nate and reminded him not to be late for the early morning present opening. This time he set his alarm for 5:30.

The morning was a repeat of the year before. Lots of laughter and teasing, as the wrapping paper was torn off and discarded in a pile. This year Molly gave Nate some thick electric socks and new gloves. It was a practical gift and nothing that Nate would view as something sentimental, so she felt it was safe.

Nate, on the other hand, had spent many countless hours carving a six-inch pine tree to go with the pinecones from last year. It was a small replica of a blue spruce, with its branches evenly spaced in the perfect conical formation it was known for. Nate was beaming and very proud of himself. The pinecones he had given her had been placed on the mantle as part of the Christmas decorations. She had said she didn't want to lose them in her dorm room. Molly placed the tree on the mantle with the pinecones and thanked Nate for his gift. Nate was oblivious to her coolness, but her family picked up on it and wondered what was bothering her. Freddy looked at his mother and raised his eyebrows in a questioning way. Cora shrugged her shoulders back in a quiet response.

Molly felt terrible and so guilty. She knew she couldn't drag on this charade any longer. She had to tell Nate about Chad. But the question was when. She just couldn't ruin his Christmas, so she decided to wait until after dinner at least, but by the time the roast chicken was being passed around, he had begun to notice the change in her. She was nervous, and didn't seem to want to look him in the eye. His body began to fill with cold dread.

After dinner, Molly made sure she was in the kitchen alone with her mother when she was cleaning up. Cora told the men to get back to their card game from last night.

"Mom, I have something to talk to you about."

"What is it, dear? Is everything all right?"

"Not exactly." Molly hesitated and her mother let the pregnant pause hang in the air. She already knew what Molly was about to say, but she wanted it to come from her first. "I don't know how to tell Nate, but I've found someone new."

Cora put down her dishcloth and led Molly to the kitchen table. "What do you mean? Tell me."

"When I went skiing in Colorado over Thanksgiving break, I met a guy named Chad Clairmont. We spent the entire time together. I'm crazy about him, Mom. We text or talk every day. I think I'm in love."

"But, Molly, you've only known him a month, and most of that time was long distance."

"Yes, but it's different than it is with Nate. There's an electricity between us. A real spark. He's handsome and smart and rich, too."

"Molly Sparks, you know better than to fall for someone just because they have money." Cora was concerned now. She had never seen this dreamy look in her daughter's eyes before. She was sure the attraction was real, but the question was would it last.

"Oh, it's not just for his money, but because of it, he's had opportunities that our family has never had. He's traveled a lot, and he's so smart. He's already out of school and working in his father's boating business in Minnesota. He has a great car, and he dresses so well. He's just wonderful."

"I don't know what to say," said her mother as she placed a hand over her daughter's. "Cars, boats, style of dress? It's not like you at all. But I suppose you have to do what you want, you're all grown up now, but just take it slow. Remember what we talked about before. There are always two sides to every person. The darker side is always masked during courtship. Be careful -- and what about Nate?"

"I'm going to tell him today. I just wanted to wait until after dinner, so can we please have a little time alone?"

Cora looked at her sadly for a few moments. "Just be kind, Molly. It's going to hurt him so much."

"Of course, I will be. I just hope I can find the right words."

But unfortunately, no further words would be necessary. Nate had been sent to the kitchen to refill the drink glasses. He had heard every last word. He stayed around the corner for a second, wondering if he should pretend he had not listened to their conversation, and just go on until Molly asked to talk to him. But he was never any good at pretending. Besides the tears were already filling his eyes, and the pain that followed was cutting him to the core. He put the tray of glasses on the hall table, grabbed his coat and left. It was not in his nature to confront her, slam a door, or to make a scene in any way, so he quietly stepped onto the porch and walked to the bunkhouse. It was a good thing it was empty, because the moment the door was closed, he released the sob he had been choking back. And then he sat on the side of his bed and stared at nothing, almost in a catatonic state. His brain would not function. Life without Molly was unthinkable.

When Molly discovered Nate was not in the house, she went straight to the bunkhouse, forming the words she knew would probably cut him to the quick. She could think of no way to soften the blow. She cared about him so much, but Chad was – well, Chad was exciting and worldly, -- and Nate was here on the tree farm.

When she got to the cabin, she knocked softly. When she didn't get an answer, she opened the door and peeked in. Nate was lying on the bed, and would not turn to look at her.

"I'll spare you the speech," he said, sadly. "I heard what you said to your mother. You're here to break up with me."

"Nate, I -- "

He sat up, but avoided her eyes. "Look, Molly, I get it. You're in college. You want to have fun, and I'm here working on a farm you detest. You're free to go with no complaints from me. I've been on my own for most of my life. Deep down, I always knew what we had was too good to be true. Most people can't be trusted, but I didn't put you in that category. I have to admit that I did truly trust you, and I believed in your promises."

"I'm so sorry. I don't know what to say."

"Just leave. I'll stay out of your way for the rest of your vacation. I'd leave right now, but I have too much respect for your family, and I know your dad needs my help in the barn this winter. Please explain to them for me why I walked out of the house."

Molly stood quietly, watching him as he stared at the floor. She felt tears prick her eyes. Hurting him was far more painful than she had anticipated. And saying goodbye had filled her with an emptiness she had never experienced before. She started to form a word, and instead turned and slowly walked out, her head hanging low. Before she closed the door, she looked at the broken man on the side of bed once more, hoping she had not made a huge mistake.

≈

The next few days were unbearable for Nate. He remained in the bunkhouse until Molly left for school, and then he came out of his self-imposed seclusion. After talking to Duane, Nate decided to stay on until spring. He needed the job, and he wanted to finish his last term at community college. When a chance to share an apartment with a school friend came up, Nate moved out so he would be gone before Molly came home for spring break. Christmas Day was the last time he saw her. He occasionally heard Duane and Freddy make some comment about her, but they tried not to talk about her in his presence. But as many times as he had tried to wipe her out of his mind, each Christmas, when talk of different types of trees to buy, how many lights to decorate with, and pinecone wreaths versus fresh bough wreaths came up, he was wounded once again.

Chapter Nine

Present Day

"Nate, do you have the Roberts claim done yet? Nate! Nate, did you hear me?"

"Oh, sorry, Bill. I wasn't paying attention. I thought I saw someone I knew," said Nate, spinning around quickly from the window.

"Well, did you?" laughed Bill Winters, the manager at the insurance firm Nate had been working at for the last ten years.

"No, I don't think so. I, uh, I didn't get a good look. Maybe."

"Something sure has you flustered. Was it a pretty lady, by any chance?"

"Just someone from my past. But I'm sure it's not her. We're a long way from the state she lives in now." Moving quickly around his desk, Nate handed Bill the folder he had been working on. "I don't see any reason why we can't pay out the full amount of the damage. Everything looks to be on the up-and-up, and the accident was not their fault."

"Okay, good. They're good customers, and I want to keep it that way. Thanks for expediting this. I appreciate it."

"No problem," said Nate, and he meant it. He was always glad to do whatever it took to make the people he worked with happy.

As Bill started to walk out of Nate's office, he turned and said, "Hey, don't forget the office party on the 23rd. It's at our house this year. You can bring a plus-one."

"Plus-one?"

"You know, a date. But I know you don't like to call it that, so I went for the more politically correct term."

"Sure, I'll be there, but I'm not dating anyone. I'll go solo." Nate fussed with some items on his desk, rearranging things in neat piles. He knew how this conversation would go. They always wanted to pair him up with someone. If he wanted a date, he could get one on his own, but this morning's memories which had come crashing down on him after looking out the window, had reminded him, it was not a good idea to get involved with anyone.

It's not that Nate was against dating girls. He was after all a healthy American male, but he usually avoided seeing the same person more than two or three times in a row. After that, most of the females he had met began to get clingy and needy. They wanted more than he was ready to give. He had been on the other end of that once, and it wasn't pretty. Falling in love was not for him – never again. He was perfectly happy going to a movie or a dinner with a woman for companionship, and if she invited him to her place, then fine, but he would never be husband material, so why bother going any further.

The night of the party, he dressed himself in casual dark grey slacks, then chose a forest green sweater. It was not the Christmas green that everyone would be wearing with their bright cardinal reds, but he was satisfied that he would fit in at least. On the way to the party, he decided to stop for a bottle of wine to take along as a hostess gift. He had learned over the years that it was always appreciated. Just as he was checking out, he caught a glimpse of a woman with wild brown curls. A man took her arm and stepped in front of her, blocking his view of her face. He caught his breath, but when they turned he could clearly see that it was not Molly. He chastised himself. Would he never get over looking for her? There could be a whole city of curly brown-haired woman for all he knew. And besides, he was in Grand Rapids now, on the other side of the state from Holly. She had gone to college in Iowa and perhaps stayed closer to that area. One time, when he was at his weakest, he had Googled her. She looked happy and in love with someone from Minnesota. They were bundled up with fur trimmed parkas, holding up a Huskie puppy. It looked like they were at a dogsled race. He had studied her face closely while blocking the man's out, then he had zoomed in on her eyes. After several moments of drowning in their depths of swirling grey colors, and feeling tortured because he could no longer read what was there, he had clicked off and never looked again.

When Nate arrived to the party, it was already in full swing. He had had a difficult time finding a place to park and had had to walk in the snow for almost a full block, but when the door was opened for him, he felt a warmth inside that was comforting. His friends were happy to see him and called out greetings. Stacy came forward to take his coat. He had not talked to her much since she had offered to go Christmas shopping with him.

"Merry Christmas, Nate," she purred. She ran her hands over his arms and kissed him on the cheek before helping him to slip off his coat. She smelled like jasmine, a scent that had always been too sweet for his taste. She lost her balance and he grabbed her arm to steady her. He laughed in a teasing way, and said, "Whoa, it looks like someone has already hit the punch bowl a little hard."

"It's a party, Nate. You're supposed to enjoy yourself. Come on, enjoy it with me."

"Sure," he said, but to stall her a little, he added, "but I want to say hello to Bill and Carol first. I'll be with you in a sec." Pulling himself away, he was hoping to get swallowed up in the crowd and lose her. She was pleasant enough, but he could already feel the beginning of her possessiveness. "Hey, Bill, Merry Christmas. Where's Carol? I brought a bottle of wine to give her."

"She's in the kitchen. I'm sure she'll be out soon. Glad you came, Nate. I see you decided to come alone. That's fine. There are several single gals here." He winked as if to say, take your pick.

"Why do I always have to have a girl on my arm? I'm capable of handling a party by myself."

"Just kidding. You're a little sensitive tonight, aren't you, pal? Here, come with me and get a drink. Maybe that will mellow you out a little."

The next hour or so, went perfectly fine, as Nate moved from group to group, chatting with his friends and co-workers. Someone handed him a tray of hors d'oeurves and said, "Would you mind taking this to the kitchen and asking Carol to refill it, please?"

"I'm sorry, I'm not a waiter. I -- "

She was weaving on her feet, and said, with a sloppy smile, "Thanks."

"Oh, okay, I guess I can do that." He laughed to himself at how foolish people could get when they were drinking. He had always had a two-drink maximum for just that reason. In Nate's mind, there was more to life than getting so drunk that you could not remember anything the next day, followed up with being sick for most of the morning. He wondered why people insisted on doing that to themselves over and over, and having been in the position of observer many times, he knew exactly how ridiculous they often looked.

As Nate neared the kitchen area which was open to the family room, he heard his name, so he stopped near the large potted palm.

"Isn't he adorable?"

"Who? Nate?" asked Carol, his boss' wife.

"Of course, silly. There's no other man out there who can compare."

"Settle down, Nancy. You're married."

"Just sayin'. Why hasn't Nate been snatched up yet?"

"I'm not sure; we've tried to pair him up quite often, but it never takes."

"You don't suppose he's -- "

"Nate? Of course not. I had someone planned out for him tonight, but she seems to be a no-show."

"Oh, you mean -- ?"

"Shh, I thought I heard something."

That was all Nate needed to hear. He turned around, put the tray on a nearby table, grabbed his coat from the rack by the door, and left. He had to stop listening in on people's conversations. It brought back a memory of that day at the Sparks' house when he had overheard Molly. It was just too much. He knew it was rude not to say goodbye to his host and hostess, but then she was in the kitchen talking about his love life. He would not let people manipulate him in any way. It seemed to be a common thread lately. 'Let's get Nate married,' was all anyone could think about. He walked out of the door, leaving a trail of Christmas carols hanging in the air, and the laughter of people enjoying the Christmas spirit together. He paused for one second and almost changed his mind, but no -- he didn't need all of this Christmas fuss. It was just another day. He would be perfectly happy to spend the evening alone.

Chapter Ten

"Mom, hurry up! You're already late."

"Don't worry. I'm okay. These things last well into the night."

Her thirteen-year-old daughter rolled her eyes and sighed. "You're stalling, and you know it. You're hoping the party will be over when you get there, and then you can just come home. Now, look at yourself in the mirror. You're gorgeous."

Molly studied herself, trying to get a view that only others would see. She turned around, looked over her shoulder, then back to the front again. "This darn hair. I can never do anything with it."

"Stop, Mom. It's perfect. I like it up like that. Hurry. You promised to drop me off at Katie's house. She's waiting."

"Okay, you're sure I look all right? I have a feeling they're trying to set me up with someone."

Maddie took her mother's hands in hers. "Mom, we talked about this. It's okay. I can handle you going on a date. Dad's been dating for years already."

"Well, that's your father. Don't get me started."

"Oops, sorry. I shouldn't have mentioned it. But when we moved here from Minnesota, you promised things would be different. It's your time now, and it's Christmas. Now go. Tomorrow we have to leave to see Grandma and Grandpa at the farm. This is your only chance to escape me for a night," her laughing daughter said.

"Sweetpea, I never want to *escape* from you."

"Just kidding." She gave her mother a gentle push toward the door. "Now let's go. Katie's waiting."

"Okay," she sighed. "Let's go."

Molly hated going to parties alone. That moment when you walk into a room of people, and everyone turns to see who just came in, was unbearable for her. There was a time when Molly was full of life; she had loved being in a crowd. But time changed things, wore her down a bit, sadness had eroded her joy away, and she could not get it through people's heads that she really didn't like parties. Freddy had found this job for her in Grand Rapids, Michigan after she lost her teaching position in St. Paul and that's where she had met Carol. Carol worked in the school office, and the minute she found out that Molly was divorced, she began talking about this 'perfect' man who would be just right for her. She was bound and determined to introduce him to Molly. He was fun and handsome, and everyone liked him, Carol had said. So Molly had finally agreed to go to Bill and Carol's party.

She had taken special care with her hair, putting it up, letting the curls fall away from her face while wisps dangled enticingly at her neck. She wore a form-fitting dark green dress with a Vee neckline, which allowed a hint of cleavage to be seen. Around her neck she had placed a new necklace she recently purchased. It was a simple gold chain with a small gold pinecone. When she first saw it, she had reached out to caress the small seedpod, feeling the ridges where seeds would be released, if it were real. Her hands began to shake, and she just had to have it. She had told Maddie that it reminded her of her youth on the tree farm, but the truth was that it had reminded her of something else – or rather *someone* else. If she was honest with herself, she would have to admit that she had thought of Nate often over the years. When things started to go bad with Chad, she would often wonder what life might have been like if she had stayed with Nate. She knew now that she had been a foolish young girl. She had chased after what she thought was a big prize, but had missed the trophy right in front of her. Leaving the comfort of the tree farm, her parents, and Holly Michigan was the worst thing she had ever done.

Molly had Googled Nate once after the divorce, and was surprised to find that he was working right here in Grand Rapids at an insurance office. She had thought about contacting him, but she knew he probably never wanted to see her again, and she didn't want to put herself through that rejection. Chad had been verbally abusive, and over time, his words had beat her into the mud and then dragged her through it. Maddie was the only good thing that ever came out of that marriage. Two years out, and moving to another state had not yet healed her wounds.

Molly pulled up in front of the highly decorated house. It was, in fact, the brightest lit home of the neighborhood. Lights trimmed the doorway and ran along the edge of the roofline. The windows were filled with a warm yellow glow from the interior lights, while candles in each window welcomed Mary and Joseph to spend the night at their house, as they waited for their child, the son of God, to be born. A wreath hung on a hook on the door. A red ribbon and bow which covered an antique sled on the porch rippled gently in the breeze. The porch railing had been draped with green pine branches and lights, presenting a welcoming entrance for all. A huge outside Christmas tree had been trimmed with all white lights. They twinkled as the snow gently landed on its branches. She could see the people inside, holding drinks and laughing. Soft Christmas music had been pumped outside, so even that was inviting, but suddenly a cold fear settled over Molly. There were too many people. It looked over-crowded. She assumed they all had a date but her. She was to be the single woman meant to pair up with the only single man. A self-proclaimed matchmaker, Carol had invited her for that very purpose, even though she did not work at Bill's firm. She said she knew the perfect man, and the Christmas party was just the right time for them to meet. Molly's heart started to beat rapidly, as she began to breathe heavily, sucking in air, but it felt as if there was none to be had. It was the start of one of her panic attacks. She had not had one since before she had moved here, but she knew that she had to take herself out of the situation that was causing it, so instead of parking the car, she drove on. She had no idea what to do next, except to head back home. She would have to face the music when Maddie challenged her decision in the morning. Her wise daughter would say she should have faced her fears, repeating the same words her very own mother had doled out to her when she was young. That's what came from having a precocious child. She grew up thinking she knew more than her parent.

On the way back to her comfortable suburb of Grandville, Molly decided to take a pass through downtown and look at the decorations. It was one of her favorite parts of the Christmas holiday, and now she had missed out because she had darted away from Bill and Carol's house like a deer in the path of an oncoming car. She needed to regain her thoughts and composure before she went home.

The streets were almost empty of traffic. She leisurely drove less than the 25-mile-per-hour speed limit and enjoyed looking in the store windows on Monroe Street. Each crosswalk had a red banner with a white pine tree on the light pole connecting the strings of overhead lights, which crisscrossed the street. Even though most people spent their money at the large mall, downtown shopping was alive and well. During the day, when the office buildings were packed with lawyers, bankers, employees of the advertising firms, and insurance agents, foot traffic was actually quite heavy, especially at lunch time. At night, the parking ramps swelled with concert goers for the Grand Rapids Symphony at DeVos Hall, and at other times excited ticket holders walked from their parking spot to see the latest traveling Broadway play. A few blocks away there was a large auditorium, the Van Andel Arena, for rock and pop concerts and hockey games. This year Molly had taken Maddie to see The Trans-Siberian Orchestra for the first time. That night was an experience mother and daughter would never forget. Grand Rapids was the second largest city in Michigan. It had all anyone could want, but it still felt like a small town.

Driving slowly through the quiet snow-covered streets, she felt a calm come over her, and she realized that she really loved it here. And when she saw an empty parking space in front of a late night coffee shop/diner, she pulled in without a second thought. Right now, more than anything, she wanted a mocha decaf. Chocolate coffee was calling her name.

Molly had forgotten how dressed up she was, but no one seemed to notice, so she slid into a booth by the window, sitting with her back to the door, and watched the snow fall silently to the already white blanket, adding more inches by the minute. A contentment flooded over her, and she noticed her breathing was back to normal; the uneven gasping for air apparently chased away by her calming Christmastime drive. She touched the pinecone necklace at her throat, and wondered where he was and what he was doing now. He was probably around the tree with his own family. Molly imagined him with a wife and two or three kids. At least one would be a little boy who looked just like him. She sighed, and was jarred out of her thoughts when the waitress asked what she could get her. When the warm cup was delivered, bringing with it a delicious coffee/chocolate aroma, she smiled to herself. Here she was, afraid of going into a party alone, and she was sitting in a diner by herself with no problem whatsoever. She realized now how silly she had been. Maybe Carol was right, and he would have been the perfect man, but now she would never know.

Nate decided to swing by his office and pick up some folders he had left there. Christmas was only two days away and on a weekend, so the office was closed now until after the holidays. He had planned to work part of the time and binge-watch some Netflix. Maybe he could finally catch up on Vikings. Watching a lot of TV was his usual Christmas past time. He would order a pizza for Christmas Eve, and then on Christmas Day he would make bacon and eggs for breakfast and eat whatever leftovers he could find for dinner and finish off any food cravings with junk food. He was perfectly fine with that, it was all he had ever known, except for the two years at the tree farm. For the most part, he tried to block that time of his life out. It had been the best time of his life, but if he thought about it too much, it hurt more than he cared to admit.

After leaving his office with his briefcase packed with work, he walked across the street to his favorite coffee shop intending to pick up some bagels and donuts to take home. The snow was falling in that lazy way it did when there was no wind. A single flake would zigzag slowly down until it landed on a spot that needed covering. He caught one of those flakes and tried to study it before it disappeared. He wished he could paint or draw or something. If he had artistic talent, he would paint nothing but snowflakes. Molly had always loved them. She said pinecones covered with snow was God's handiwork. He tensed. Why had he been thinking of her so often after all of this time? An ache in his gut almost made him bend over. It had been sixteen years since he had seen her last and yet the pain was still so raw. He took a deep breath and shook his head to clear his thoughts, and then he pushed the door open to the shop.

Nate walked back to his favorite booth, and as he passed the counter, Dave the barista called out. "Hey, what are you doing here? Didn't you have a party to go to?"

"Yeah, I ditched it. Can I get my usual for here? I think I'll sit a while, and then I'll get one to go. And wrap up two bagels and a half-dozen donuts for me."

"You got it."

Molly was so engrossed in her thoughts that she had not even noticed when the man passed her booth and sat in the one next to hers. He seated himself facing the door so he was looking right at a woman, with her chin in her left hand, as she stared out the window. He froze. His mind must be playing tricks. First the woman out his window, then the one in the store, and now -- it couldn't possibly be. But this time it was her, and he wondered why he had even questioned it. 'Molly,' he almost said aloud. She hadn't changed in the least in the last sixteen years. She looked exactly as he had last seen her, with her curls escaping the up-do at the nape of her neck. If only he could see her eyes.

He watched her for a bit, studying the lines of her face and the gentle curls that framed it. She was beautiful. His heart was full of joy at seeing her again, and at the same time a sharp ache forced its way through. He noticed that she was wearing a ring on her left hand, but it did not look like a wedding ring. It was dark blue, possibly a sapphire birthstone ring or just a pretty gemstone. Yes, her birthday was in September. He exhaled loudly, suddenly relieved that she was not married, but immediately he felt her pain and sorrow. What had gone wrong? Did she divorce? Had he passed away? Too many years had gone by for her to have remained single.

Molly was suddenly aware that she was being watched. She pulled her eyes away from the window and looked across her table at a man looking back. It took only a fraction of a second for her to recognize the very man she had been thinking about, but she wasn't sure if she was still in her daydream or if this was reality. And then she heard his voice.

"Molly?"

"Nate?" Her heart was pounding so hard she could barely hear her own voice.

"Oh, my goodness, Molly. Wh — what are you doing here?" He got up from the booth so quickly that he cracked his knee on the table top. She began to slide out of her booth to meet him halfway.

"Nate, I can't believe it's you!"

"Molly, it's so good to see you." He reached for her hands and held them in his. It felt so good to touch her again.

"Oh, Nate, it's really you!" Then she did a miraculous thing. She wrapped her arms around him for a hug; he pulled her in closer than she had expected. The contact was shocking at first, but it immediately felt right and she allowed it. They were both suddenly aware that they were in a public place. Molly blushed. "Please sit with me. Can you stay a while?"

"I have nowhere else to go, so yes, I would love to sit with you."

The two old friends and former lovers sat there like school children grinning at each other. The barista was grinning himself, along with a few other customers who couldn't help but feel the joy along with them.

Finally Nate was able to ask a few question. "You look great, Molly. I mean it." He wanted to say she was the most beautiful woman he had ever seen, but he held back from expressing all of his thoughts. He had learned that lesson well.

"Thanks, Nate. So do you." Molly blushed again. She could feel the heat rise up her neck, and it wasn't like her. She placed her hand on her necklace in an effort to distract him from seeing her turn red, but all it did was call attention to the necklace itself.

"A pinecone?"

"Ah, yes, I just bought it the other day. It reminded me of home, I guess. You know, the tree farm."

He wondered if it had reminded her of other things. The way they were together back then. How easy it was for them. "Tell me about yourself. Are you married? Kids?"

"I was married to Chad — you know. But that ended two years ago. It wasn't so bad though, because it gave me Maddie, my thirteen-year-old daughter."

"Wow, thirteen. It's hard to imagine you as a mother to a teenager." But what he was really thinking was 'good, she's not married.' He said instead, "Anyone special in your life?"

She sucked in a breath and then laughed. "I have not dated since I went through the divorce. Tonight was supposed to be my first time out, but I bailed. I was supposed to go to a Christmas party and meet someone there, but I left them hanging. That's the reason I'm so dressed up. I feel so awful," she laughed.

"Really? That's funny, because I was at a Christmas party where I had discovered I was being set up, so I slipped out." They laughed together and it felt good.

"Wait," said Nate. "My date never showed, or at least had not yet arrived when I left. What party were you going to?"

"My friend Carol's, from work. It was her husband Bill's work party. She insisted I come, because she wanted me to meet someone."

"You don't mean Bill and Carol Winters?" asked Nate beginning to put some pieces together.

"Yes, that's them. You don't mean -- "

They burst out laughing. "We were supposed to meet at the party. They had set us up, and we both ran." Tears were streaming down Molly's face. Nate could barely catch his breath.

"How strange is that? Of course, they had no idea we already knew each other." Nate shook his head, marveling at the coincidence. "Wait, why are you here? I mean not only here, in this coffee shop at almost midnight right before Christmas, but why are you in Grand Rapids?"

"Oh, I moved here two years ago, after my divorce. I wanted to leave the area anyway, and so

Freddy found out that there was a teaching position available at a private school near his home, and he notified me of the opening. I applied and I got it. As far as this place, it was pure accident. I was just driving aimlessly through the city looking at the lights, and decided to stop, something I never do alone."

"Amazing. So you're a teacher. Well, I guess I knew that, already. I have to admit that I Googled you once. That's fantastic. I can see that you would do well in that job."

Pleased that he had tried to look her up, she continued, "But what about you? Why are you here?"

"Well, my office is across the street. I come here often. After I left the party, I stopped in to work to pick up some folders, and decided to grab some coffee and donuts for the weekend. As you might remember, I stay home for Christmas, and I needed to bulk up my junk food."

"So, there's no one to go home to?" she shyly asked.

"No, there's no one. There have been a few girls here and there who were special, but I've never been married." He ached to say, there was never anyone but you for me.

"Oh, I see. Well, um, I guess that's good, right? Um, do you think this was just a coincidence, purely an accident that we met here? Or part of a bigger plan?" She looked into his eyes, now braver than before since she knew he was unattached.

"I think it was meant to be, pure and simple. If we had met at the party, it would have been the plan, but since we both took matters into our own hands, God took over and worked it out for us. You have no idea how happy I am to see you."

"Me, too, Nate." They held hands across the table and lost track of all time, as they reminisced about old times and caught each other up on their lives. When Dave called out that they were about to close, they were both shocked at how the time had passed.

"Oh my goodness. I have to get home. I had no idea it was so late." She began to gather her scarf and purse, but he reached for her hands again.

"Can I see you again? Soon?"

"I'd like that."

"Tomorrow?"

"I would have said yes, but I'm going to the farm to see my parents. We always go for Christmas Eve and stay over for Christmas morning." She saw the look of disappointment cross his eyes, and without thinking further she said, "Come with us."

"What?"

"Yeah, why not? Freddy will be there, with his wife and kids, and I go with my daughter. My folks would love to see you. Mom brings you up every now and then."

"She does?" he felt tears prick his eyes.

"Yes," Molly chuckled, "she tried real hard to get me to look you up after the divorce."

"Why didn't you?"

Her face changed to a sober expression, one Nate had not remembered seeing on her before. "I was embarrassed at my failure, I guess. I was embarrassed at how much I had hurt you, and I was embarrassed that I had made such a colossal mistake."

"You think it was a mistake?" he asked softly.

"Yes, of course, it was. Even my own daughter tells me so."

"You told her about me?"

"She knows everything about you, and she's been in cahoots with her grandmother to get me to take this step for two years. Please, come with us. She'll be so pleased; she's always wanted to meet you. I know you'll be alone and even though you say that's how you like it, you really don't. Christmas means more to you than you care to admit, Nate Finnegan."

It may have looked to Molly as though he was mulling over what he should do, but Nate could not truly believe what had just happened. Not only had they met in a bizarre way after all of these years, but she was asking him to go back to the family farm, the one place where he had felt the happiest in his entire life. The only place where Christmas had meant something to him. His slowly emerging smile turned to a grin that spread across his face as he said, "Yes, I'll go. What time do we leave?"

Chapter Eleven

On the morning of the 24th, Nate popped out of bed at 6:00. He heated a cup of his leftover coffee in the microwave and popped into the shower, where he sang Deck the Halls at the top of his lungs. He couldn't believe this day was actually going to happen. The many small coincidences converging into an 'accidental' meeting with Molly at the coffee shop, and the fact that she was available, and the fact that she wanted to take him to her family's home today, and the fact that her daughter already knew about him and had encouraged it, was way more than chance. With tears merging into the shower water, he closed his eyes and said a prayer of thanks to God above for granting him another opportunity to make things right.

"Oh, man," said Nate out loud. "I don't have any gifts. Hurry, you can do it," he said encouraging himself to pick up his speed.

By seven o'clock he was at the local Walgreen's which was open 24 hours a day, 7 days a week. Almost running up and down the aisles, he was able to grab some boxes of candy for Freddy's teenagers, not knowing their ages or sex, candy seemed to be the best bet – he thought Molly had said there were three, but he took an extra one just in case. He bought a small ceramic gingerbread house/music box for Freddy and Claire as a couples' gift. He found a nice bottle of gin for Duane, since he remembered how he loved his gin and tonics at Christmas time, and he found some pretty Christmas place mats for Cora, with a matching oven mitt and kitchen towel. Then to the jewelry and makeup counter for Molly's daughter. He remembered Molly had said she was thirteen, so when he spotted a variety of nail polish colors in a pretty Christmas tin, he grabbed it. Now for Molly. What to get Molly. He had known her so well at one time, but how much had she changed? He had no idea what her house looked like. Was she into contemporary, country, antiques? He stopped dead in his tracks and decided to take his time for this one. This gift had to be just right. He slowly began to walk the aisles, his small basket overloaded, now heavy and awkward to carry. When he found himself in the Christmas tree trimming aisle, he saw how limited the choices were, having been well picked over by now. He tripped over a box which had been left in the aisle, and as he fell forward slightly, his eyes came right in line with the perfect item. He reached out carefully to take it off the shelf hook. It was a hand-blown pinecone tree ornament, a delicate glass replica of the ones he had carved for her. It had been painted in a warm bronze color, with tiny sparkles glued sparingly over it, so it looked as if it had been sprinkled with fresh new snow glittering in the moonlight. Nate's hand shook. Not so much at this perfect Christmas gift, but at what it could mean. Would she see it the same way he had? Would she see the promises that had gone along with pinecones in the past and then weren't fulfilled? Would she see it as pressure to get back together? Was it too much too soon? These were the questions he was asking himself in the center of an all-night pharmacy. He laughed at how ridiculous it all seemed.

And then a small little voice in his head said, "If you don't try, you will never know how she feels. You don't have her now, and haven't for the past sixteen years. Do it, you fool. Give love another chance."

"YES," he said out loud, then he quickly glanced around to see if anyone was nearby. No, he was the only 'fool' in the store at seven o'clock in the morning on Christmas Eve day. He ran to the checkout, but not before grabbing some wrapping paper, tape, and gift cards. The clerk was laughing at his infectious excitement, and after bagging everything up, she wished him a Merry Christmas. He almost wanted to kiss her when he heard those words. His heart was so full of excitement he thought it would burst. Christmas! It was Christmas!

Text Molly for status of arrival – check. Pack overnight bag – check. Wrap presents – check. Place all gifts in a tote bag – check. Take warm hat, boots, and gloves – check. Turn off all appliances – check. Leave house in a mess – check. Well, the last one wasn't on his list, but it should have been. There were scraps of wrapping paper, ribbons, and bows, everywhere. Gift wrapping had never been his strong suit. He would deal with the mess when he returned.

When he heard her car horn toot, he jumped up nervously, smoothing his hair, grabbing his coat and gloves, and then locking the door behind him. Now, he only hoped her daughter liked him. If not, the two-hour ride could be miserable.

"Now, remember, Maddie, be polite."

"Of course, mother," she rolled her eyes.

"Will you get in the back seat, please? It might be strange if we make *him* ride in the back."

"Okay. But I know you just want to be closer to him," teased her daughter.

"Maddie, please. I'm nervous enough as it is."

"Relax, Mom. It will all be fine. Oh, here he comes."

"Hi, Nate. So glad you could make it," said Molly. "Let me pop the trunk so you can put your bag in there along with our stuff." When she glanced in the tote and saw Christmas gifts, she was shocked. "Oh, Nate, you didn't have to buy us anything, and besides, how did you have time?"

"My little secret. And I wanted to. I haven't wanted to, since – well, since – you know, the last time."

Molly touched his hand, aching for the pain she had caused him. She would have loved to kiss him right now, but Maddie was trying to see what was going on at the back of the car, and luckily the raised trunk obstructed her view or she would have seen the glances passing between the two. "Come on, let's get in. It's cold out. I'm so glad we have good roads today, aren't you?"

The two-hour road trip passed quickly. Maddie was a delightful girl, funny, chatty, and eager to see her mother happy. She engaged in conversation with Nate, answering his questions about school, and returning questions of her own about his job, music he liked, and which sports he watched. She had been warned not to ask about his family. Molly couldn't have been more pleased with her daughter.

After texting her mother early this morning, saying she was bringing a surprise guest who would be staying overnight with them, Molly contacted Freddy to tell him the news. Freddy had known that Nate was somewhere in the Grand Rapids area, but with a busy life of his own, and fear of hurting Molly, he had not contacted Nate in any way. But now he couldn't wait to see him.

As Molly's car neared the farmhouse, Nate rolled down the window, and breathed in the fresh scent of pine and snow. He had forgotten how much he loved that smell. Freddy's car was there already, which surprised Molly. Usually, he was the last one to arrive. Trying to get three teenaged children to move at the same time was a chore, but everyone had been eager to find out who the mystery man was that their aunt was bringing to the family gathering, so it hadn't taken as much prodding as normal.

Nate hopped out, heading towards the back of the car, ready to help carry in the gifts and food from the trunk, but Molly tugged at his hand and said, "Let's do that in a minute. We'll go in and say hello first, okay?"

Suddenly his heart was racing. This was the family that he had wanted for his very own. This was the day he had dreamed of. Arriving at Christmastime with a car full of gifts, being greeted by those who loved him, hugs and kisses all around. This was the day. Today would decide his fate. He wondered how they would receive him. He wondered if Molly was just being nice, or was she ready to try again. Everything hinged on how people reacted when he opened that door. Molly could feel his nerves as she tugged at his hand.

"Come on, you two," yelled Maddie. "Grandma's probably dying to know who is coming."

Maddie raced to the door, opened it with a crash, and yelled, "We're here."

Much to Nate's surprise, the entire family was waiting to greet him. Standing in a row like a reception line. They later learned that Freddy's youngest had spilled the beans after overhearing a conversation between his parents. When Nate walked in, everyone yelled "Merry Christmas!" and then it was hugs and back slaps all around. Cora wiped her eyes, feeling as though a long lost son had returned home.

"We missed you, Nate," she whispered.

"I missed you all more than I can say," he whispered back.

"Good to see you, buddy," said Freddy.

"Welcome home, son" added Duane, then he yelled, "Don't just stand there with the door open. Were you raised in a barn?" It was a standard phrase he had said often to the kids when they were young because they never closed a door behind them. The joke was that they *had* practically been raised in a barn.

"Oh, Dad. You'll never change," Molly replied. "Freddy, will you help Nate get the things out of the car? Thanks."

Cora tugged at Molly's hands as the kids ran off to look at the tree in the living room. "Come into the kitchen. You, too, Claire. Molly, tell me everything, quick before they get back."

Molly laughed, "Well, it's quite a story, coincidence, led by God's hand. But the gist of it is, that we accidentally ran into each other at a coffee shop last night and couldn't stop talking, and you know Nate. He didn't have anywhere to go for Christmas, same as always, so I invited him to come home with me."

"Still?" said Cora. "I'm surprised. I would have thought he would be married with a family by now."

"He's never married. No kids."

Claire grinned, "I knew it. No one else compared. He was always waiting for you. How romantic," she squealed.

"Oh, Claire."

The Christmas Eve supper was a light meal meant to appeal to the kids, but the grownups were just as happy with the fare. Barbeque sandwiches, potato chips and dip, pickles and olives and baked beans, and, of course, lots of cookies and fudge. Then the whole group drove to church for the Christmas Eve service. It was exactly as Nate had remembered. He reached over to squeeze Molly's hand, when they sang Silent Night in candlelight, just as he had done the last time he came here with the family. When she smiled at him, he could have sworn he saw tears glistening in her eyes. Then it was home for some hot chocolate before bed. The house was crowded with family, and the bedroom arrangements had already been established before he was invited. The teens all slept on the floor by the fireplace in their sleeping bags. Duane apologized to Nate that he was to be sent away from the house, but the only place left with an empty bed was the bunkhouse where he used to live. He was thrilled. Cora had had just enough time after Molly's call to put some fresh bedding on the cot and stoke up the fire so the building was warm. He would be the only one staying there tonight, as there was only one hired hand left, and he had gone home.

Molly walked Nate to the cabin, holding his hand as they went. It seemed as though the last sixteen years had never happened, now that they were back in this familiar setting. The way Nate looked at her made her feel young and beautiful again, something she hadn't felt in years. Her heart was skipping beats like she was a love sick teenager.

"Molly, thanks for asking me here. I really love your family and the way they celebrate Christmas. I always have."

"And they love you."

Nate hesitated for a moment before he started to speak. "You know, I haven't been happy at my job. I always knew that office work wasn't for me, but I didn't know what else to do with my life when I left here. I have something to say, but I don't want it to jeopardize anything that we might have going."

"What is it?"

"Your Dad was telling me that he wants to retire."

"Yes, he talks of it now and then, but recently it seems like he means it."

Nate exhaled slowly, wondering if he should say it, because his very future was at stake. "He said that Freddy is not interested in running Pine Haven Tree Farm, and he plans on selling."

"Really? I didn't know he had gone that far with his plan. I'm not sure I like that idea, but what else can they do?"

"He seems very serious. It might sound quick, but I have thought about this for years. I want to buy it, Molly. But --"

"You're afraid it will chase me away."

"Yes, and I just found you again."

"Look, Nate, I love this place. I love the country smells, the fresh air, and small town living. I even love the house and barn. I just don't want to *work* on a farm. I'm a teacher now, and I love it. But don't let that stop you from whatever you want to do with your life. I think Dad would be happy to see you take it over."

They were quiet for a few moments as Nate thought about what she had just said. He could not live out his life in an enclosed building, solving problems for people he had never met, but he could not imagine going on without her. "I think I'd like to make an offer. I would let him and your mother live in the house until they no longer wanted to, or they pass on. Time doesn't matter. I'd fix up the bunkhouse for my own little cottage. I can be very happy out here. And, that way, if I'm lucky, I can see you once in a while."

There was a heavy silence for a moment as they both remembered the way it once was between them. They had arrived at the bunkhouse, which gave Nate something to do to break the awkwardness between them. He fumbled with the lock to the door while Molly stood by watching the way his jaw line worked as he concentrated on his task. She suddenly wanted to reach out and stroke his cheek; she yearned to feel the late night bristles that were beginning to appear on his face. At last the door opened. "It seems to be sticky. I guess it could use a little TLC. The whole place could, actually. Um – would you like to step in for a minute?" he asked, as he pulled off his hat and unzipped his parka, giving him a reason to avoid her eyes

"Sure, just for a minute, though. They'll wonder where I went."

"Here, let me light this lantern; your mom said the electricity is not on out here, anymore."

"Dad's been trying to save on the budget, I guess."

When he struck a match to the oil lamp, the room filled with a warm golden glow. Nate watched as shadows played on Molly's hair; her grey eyes illuminated brightly when she saw how he was looking at her. Nate stepped forward, no longer able to contain himself, "Molly, I --"

"Shh," she whispered, placing her fingers on his lips. "Don't say it. It was never your fault. I made a terrible mistake. I was young and stupid. And after the first year of marriage, it was difficult to admit it to myself, but I knew I should never have chosen anyone else but you."

"I pushed you too hard. You weren't ready. I should have gone slower. I --"

Molly stepped closer. She could feel the heat from his body, she opened his jacket and placed her hands on his chest, and slowly slid them up to wrap around his neck, pulling him toward her as she lifted herself on her toes. In one fluid movement, the two came together in a passion that Molly had never felt from anyone before; not even when she thought she had loved her husband. Nate tucked her into his chest, her arms now around his waist, as the jacket wrapped them like a blanket. Their kiss seemed to last an eternity, but even then, it was over too soon for Molly.

Breathing heavily, Nate finally pulled back. "I don't want to make the same mistake again."

"You won't. You never could." And she pulled him to her once more. Reality quickly set in, knowing there was a daughter waiting for her, and parents who would expect an explanation if she were to stay the night. "But I do have to go back to the house."

"Do you want me to walk you back?" asked Nate with a muffled voice, while he was tasting her neck.

That made Molly laugh. "Silly, I just walked you out here."

"Well, at least take the four-wheeler back. I'll walk to the house in the morning."

"Okay, I'll agree to that. But don't be late. We have kids who will be up at the crack of dawn."

"Yes, ma'am. I'll be there before anyone is awake."

"Well, that might be too early. I'll text as soon as I put my feet on the floor. And remember, come in your pj's."

"What pj.s?" he growled. "I don't wear pajamas."

Molly pushed him away once again. "I'm looking forward to seeing what you *do* wear."

"Or don't," he said with a wink. And it was 'déjà vu all over again,' as Yogi Berra once famously said.

She slapped him playfully and closed the door, stepping into the cold dark night and leaving Nate wanting more, but exuberantly happy.

Just like the first Christmas morning on the farm seventeen years ago, Nate's phone began to vibrate with a reminder to get out of bed. He quickly brushed his teeth, ran a comb through his hair, and pulled on his sweats. Then he bundled up for the short walk to the house. When he arrived, Cora was in the kitchen making her special hot cocoa. He peeked into the living room and noticed his set of hand-carved pinecones and pine tree on the mantle. Just knowing that she had saved them, made him feel good. The youngest of Freddy's sons was already sitting next to the tree, trying to look at tags on the gifts. No one had even noticed that he had come in, so he went into the living room and sat by the boy. They were caught in the act of picking up packages and shaking them to see if they could figure out what was inside. Cora scolded them, and they both laughed with embarrassment. Nate felt like a naughty little kid. It felt good.

Molly came into the room with Maddie. They were wearing matching pajamas of a green and white pattern of Christmas songs and bells. The rest of the family came in one at a time until they were all seated by the tree. Nate could not wipe the grin off of his face. Molly sat next to him, and right in front of everyone, she gave him a quick kiss on the mouth.

"Merry Christmas, Nate."

"Merry Christmas, Molly." He glanced at Maddie to see if she was upset, but she was too busy with her cousins to even care.

The handing out of gifts and unwrapping was even more raucous than it had been the last time he was here. Having kids in the mix had really livened things up. At times an adult had to settle them down, but Nate was loving every minute of the noise and giggles of joy.

When the time came for Nate to give Molly her gift, he was worried. That pinecone represented so much to him, and he was hoping it meant the same thing to her. He was sure that the pinecone she wore meant more to her than just a reminder of her parents' farm and her life growing up on it. He prayed the gift would bring back memories to her of their promises so long ago. Molly opened her gift carefully, after Nate explained that it was breakable. Her reaction was not what he was expecting, at all. The minute she saw it, she began to laugh. "It's so sweet. Thank you. Will you help me place it on the tree?"

Puzzled, he stood next to her and hung it on the branch she had pointed out to him. "Why so high?" he asked.

"Because we need to make room for this." And she handed him her gift.

The family was busy trying to figure out what was going on, when Nate laughed at his gift in the same way she had. "The same pinecone ornament. I can't believe it."

"I stopped at an all-night pharmacy near my house on my way home from the coffee shop, not expecting to find anything good and there it was."

"Walgreen's? I went to one near me early yesterday morning."

He took her hand as they placed his ornament on the tree together. The adults watched what they were doing, knowing something special was happening, and even the kids were silent. When Nate kissed Molly, there were several that said, "Ewww."

After Christmas dinner, when the table was cleared and everyone was playing games, Molly and Nate found themselves alone by the tree, admiring their ornaments once again.

Molly surprised Nate by saying, "You know, Nate, I've been thinking. I'm not opposed to being a country school teacher, as long as I can teach, I'm happy. And

I think Maddie could use some of these old-fashioned values. I'd like to get her out of the city. She needs to be around her grandparents more as they get older, and I know they would like it. They didn't see enough of her while she was growing up."

"What are you saying?" Almost afraid of the answer she was about to give, he held his breath and prayed for the best.

"I'm saying, I'm ready to fulfill my promise to you, if you'd like me to. I'm ready to move on with my life. I'm ready to be happy again."

Nate sucked in his breath, his heart beating so loudly he could hardly hear himself speak. He needed to hear her say it out loud. There could not be any more misunderstandings. "What promise is that, Molly?"

"The one where I said I would marry you someday," she said shyly.

"I'm not sure about that."

"What? But I thought --" she sputtered.

Nate looked at the tears forming in her eyes, and decided he had to put her out of her misery. "I can't wait for someday." He dropped to one knee, and without a second thought, he asked, "Will you marry me? Soon, I mean, not someday."

Molly had never done anything so impulsive in her life as what she was about to do. Her days of waffling were over. For the first time, she was absolutely sure of what she wanted. Her next sentence was sixteen years late in coming, "Yes, yes, yes! I'll marry you."

Nate jumped up and twirled her around, not realizing he had let out a "Whoo hoo!" They wrapped their arms around each other, totally unaware that the entire family was watching, until someone picked up a cinnamon pinecone from the bowl on the hall table and tossed it at them. And then another flew at them and another.

"Congratulations and Merry Christmas," they all called, one after the other.

"Merry Christmas! Merry, Merry Christmas," responded Nate, and for the first time in his life, he truly meant it.

∞

I hope you enjoyed my first Christmas novella. It was such fun to write. Look for more Christmas stories to come, and don't forget to follow my other books, which are listed at the front of this book. Please take a moment to leave a review at Amazon.com or Goodreads.com. It is always so appreciated.

Thank you,

Jane O'Brien